Ella's Promise

(Great War – Great Love

Book Three)

A Novel

by Ellen Gable

Full Quiver Publishing
Pakenham, Ontario

This book is a work of fiction. Characters and incidents are products of the author's imaginations. Real events and characters are used fictitiously. The POW officers' camps as described in this book are fictitious.

Ella's Promise
(Great War - Great Love: Book 3)
Copyright 2019 Ellen Gable

Published by
Full Quiver Publishing
PO Box 244
Pakenham, Ontario K0A 2X0
www.fullquiverpublishing.com

ISBN Number: 978-1-987970-05-0
Printed and bound in the USA
Cover design: James Hrkach, Ellen Hrkach
Cover model photo: James Hrkach
Background photo credit: Platteboone (iStock)

NATIONAL LIBRARY OF CANADA
CATALOGUING IN PUBLICATION

Published by FQ Publishing
A Division of Innate Productions

Dedicated to the memory of my sister
Diane E. Gable "Di"
Dec. 24, 1956 – March 7, 2019
Requiescat in pace

And to Dexter James Gareth Hrkach
our first grandchild

NB: The Woman's Medical College of Pennsylvania (and not Women's) is correct because this is the way it was spelled in the first part of the 20th century.

Books by Ellen Gable

Great War Series

Julia's Gifts,
Finalist 2019 IAN Awards
Charlotte's Honor
Ella's Promise

Emily's Hope, IPPY Honorable Mention 2006
In Name Only (O'Donovan Family #1) winner, IPPY Gold Medal, 2010
A Subtle Grace (O'Donovan Family #2) finalist, IAN 2015
Stealing Jenny (bestseller with nearly 300,000 downloads on Kindle)
Come My Beloved: Inspiring Stories of Catholic Courtship
Image and Likeness: Literary Reflections
on the Theology of the Body (with Erin McCole Cupp)
Dancing on Friday, The Story of Ida Gravelle

Contributor to:

Word by Word: Slowing Down With The Hail Mary
edited by Sarah Reinhard
Catholic Mom's Prayer Companion
by Lisa Hendey and Sarah Reinhard
God Moments II: Recognizing the Fruits of the Holy Spirit
God Moments III: True Love Leads to Life
edited by Michele Bondi Bottesi
After Miscarriage: A Catholic Woman's Companion to
Healing and Hope edited by Karen Edmisten
Motherhood Matters Study Guide
(editor and contributor)
By Dorothy Pilarski

"All blood runs red."
Painted on the side of the plane flown by
Eugene Bullard in World War I

*"We are citizens of this world. The tragedy
of our times is that we do not know this."*
Woodrow Wilson

*"Every time we look at the Blessed Sacrament,
our place in heaven is raised forever."*
St. Gertrude

Chapter One
A Trained Nurse

May 22, 1918,
Le Tréport, France

Waves splashed against her bare feet as she strolled along the beach. She breathed in deeply of the fresh ocean scent that reminded her of the shore back home in the states. The English Channel wasn't an ocean, but it certainly smelled like one.

A warm breeze caressed her cheeks. Ella Christine Neumann stopped and lifted her chin, reveling in the sun's heat. On days like this, she could easily forget that the world was in the middle of a great war. Glancing up at the cliff and toward the area of the base hospital at Le Tréport, the top of the building reminded her that she would have to report for her shift in an hour.

Two men strolled the beach ahead of her. She passed a group of children playing in the sand as their mothers sat on a blanket nearby.

Ella pictured herself horseback riding at the Pennsylvania ranch when she was younger. She found nothing more satisfying than to be galloping with the wind blowing her hair and the high-grass field gliding along underneath her. When her parents could no longer afford the lessons, it broke her heart.

She touched the St. Gertrude medal on her necklace, a medal she'd received from her mother when she turned twelve. "Always pray for the Holy Souls, Ella," she had told her. "Recite the prayer of St. Gertrude."

She quietly prayed as she ambled along the beach.

Her mother, in her last letter, had asked when Ella would return home. Mama already knew the answer. "I'll come back when the war is over," she'd told her parents the day she'd left home.

However, she hadn't yet told her parents that she was planning to stay after the end of the war to gain more experience in nursing. Both her parents had been born in Germany and did not like the fact that the United States was fighting their native country. She had reminded them that she was not fighting – only helping – soldiers. To her, it didn't matter whether they were Allied or enemy. Each one was a human being who needed help.

The letters from her father and younger brother, however, were what kept her amused and connected to her family. Of her four younger siblings, her sixteen-year-old dark-haired brother, Frank, always made her laugh. Her twenty-one-year-old sister, Rosa, blond like Ella, was beautifully elegant, married and already had a child on the way. Then there were the two youngest, dark-haired Frida and blond Maria, ages twelve and ten. Frida was the family peacemaker, and Maria was the typical spoiled youngest child, who always seemed to get what she wanted. Ella missed them a great deal because they would be the most changed when she returned after a year away.

The hum of a low-flying plane brought her to the present and stopped her in her tracks. The engine of this one carried a different sound. Rarely did Le Tréport see or hear planes unless they were Allied planes. Ella stared upward and turned toward the noise as the plane flew parallel to the beach. From where she stood, it grew larger and louder by the second until a large black cross-like shape became visible. A long trail of smoke billowed from its tail as the plane appeared to be heading towards the deeper blue water beside the steep cliff two hundred feet away.

Ella froze, the scene playing like a motion picture in front of her.

The enemy plane was veering away from the beach as if steering toward the water – a man with a conscience.

Just as the plane nosedived into the water, it exploded. A gust of wind and the roar of the explosion knocked Ella flat on the sand as bits and pieces of the plane showered down upon the beach.

Mind reeling, she flung her arms over her head for protection. The few people on the beach were also flat against the ground and covering their heads. The high-pitched screams of a toddler rang out over the hum of the fire rising from the crashed plane in the water. A small girl ran past her, her face covered in blood.

Ella pulled herself up and ran toward the child, scooping her up in her arms. Dark blood ran down the girl's stringy hair, the metallic odor filling Ella's senses. A superficial shrapnel wound was bleeding – as head wounds often do – profusely. Ella reached inside her apron pocket for her headscarf and pressed it to the child's head. "Shhh, it'll be all right, little one." She pulled back the headscarf to see the extent of the damage. It was deep but probably not deep enough to need stitches. The girl finally calmed, and a frantic woman snatched her from Ella's arms without a *merci*. Her headscarf disappeared with the child.

More people from the nearby houses flooded onto the beach. No one else seemed to be injured, so Ella made her way to the *funiculaire* to return to the base hospital.

She peered out the window of the tram. The fire and smoke from the plane rose like a hand reaching for the clouds.

Ella wasn't due to work for a half hour, but she decided to walk to the main building to see where her supervisor wanted her to work. She passed the beautiful Le Trianon Hotel, now a British stationary hospital, and daydreamed what it might've been like to stay at this hotel before it became a war hospital. She'd never actually been inside, but she'd heard others speaking about the luxurious high ceilings, marble statues, running water, and bright electric lights.

With a post office, a cinema, dining huts, laundry tents, street signs and a YMCA, the base hospital here at Le Tréport was a small city in itself. Hundreds of sturdy, canvas dormitory, cooking and dining tents surrounded the main building, which was actually composed of seven long, narrow, and more permanent, steel structures. The hotel itself was perched on a hill near the *funiculaire* entrance.

Just as she approached the main building, a siren rang out indicating incoming wounded.

Her role here was supposed to be different from many of her fellow American volunteers who were untrained and inexperienced. Not only was she a trained nurse, but she had attended The Woman's Medical College of Pennsylvania for a half year – in surgical training, in particular – but her parents had asked her to quit in order to help support the family. Besides, they told her that she "couldn't be both a doctor and a wife and mother."

She begged to differ. She made a promise to herself that she would pursue a medical degree when the war was over. Financially, she wasn't sure how she would do it. If she had to choose between being a surgeon/physician or being a wife/mother, she would choose to be a physician. As much as she'd like to marry someday and have children, there was nothing stopping her from pursuing her medical degree after the war. Besides, she'd had no prospects for a husband thus far and, at her age, there likely wouldn't be.

Ella stepped into the midst of the main building's foyer as newly-wounded soldiers were being prepared for surgery.

A shrill voice shouted an order in her direction. "Miss Neumann, we don't need you here. You are assigned to the POW barrack until further notice. Besides, you speak their language."

Disappointed by the command, Ella turned to face her supervisor.

The thin, elderly nurse waved her hand dismissively and scowled. Sr. Nora was an American – like Ella – but unlike Ella, Sr. Nora had spent the last thirty years in Britain working as a nurse.

Quick to comply, Ella turned and marched away. Why did that woman despise her?

She raced across the camp toward the prisoner-of-war tent that housed the captured enemy soldiers and officers. Her dormitory barrack was on the way, so she stopped and retrieved another headscarf.

On the one hand, she appreciated that the POW barrack was closer to her sleeping quarters. On the other hand, she would willingly walk miles to work in an actual medical capacity.

She entered the barrack. This was one of the larger barracks with a higher ceiling and a latrine and running water inside. At present, only half of the cots held wounded men. She walked to the desk and perused the patients' names and conditions.

While most of these prisoners of war were not terminal, all *were* men in need of care. And since her parents had spoken German during her formative years, she was bilingual. She also learned to speak French passably since she had arrived three months ago.

Many of the men in this tent were blond and blue-eyed like Ella. But her curly hair often caused strangers to think she was of Irish descent.

The quiet din of this barrack contrasted starkly with the noise on the beach. She promised herself that she would no longer complain about working in the POW barrack. She was alive, and she was grateful for that.

Chapter Two
Disguised

This barrack feels like the inside of an oven. Major Gerhard Schmidt of the German Army unbuttoned his shirt, the stuffy air reaching his sweaty neck and chest. He was about to take it off when the young female volunteer stepped into the barrack.

He stared at the girl as she moved from bed to bed, a blond curl peeking out from under the back of the white headscarf, kindness sparkling in her blue eyes. She was attractive, but that wasn't what made him notice her. Yesterday, he studied how she interacted with the POWs. Her uniform indicated that she was American, but she lacked the bitter attitude that many Americans, Brits, and other Allies – even the medical personnel – held for the German prisoners of war.

He avoided eye contact as she approached him.

"Major Schmidt?"

He lifted his chin and stared at the most beguiling blue eyes he had ever seen.

"Do you need medicine for pain?" she asked in German.

He shook his head. *"Nein, danke."*

"You certainly have a high tolerance for pain, sir," she stated as a matter of fact, again in flawless German.

"An advantageous attribute when one is fighting in a war," he replied in German.

Rolf, his comrade in the cot next to him, shouted in German, "Catch!"

He turned. Rolf tossed a book his way. Gerhard had to lift his arms to catch it. The girl ducked to avoid being hit.

He apologized to the girl, but she didn't respond, her gaze riveted to his right shoulder. His unbuttoned shirt had slipped off his shoulder when he lifted his arms to catch the book. Glancing down, he yanked his shirt over his shoulder and buttoned it. He despised his large, hairy, brown birthmark.

"Interesting place for a birthmark," she said in German.

"Annoying," he responded in German.

She gave him a charming smile, then she moved on to Rolf's cot. He listened as she spoke again in German. Rolf, being a ladies' man, began conversing with her, asking her what a pretty girl like her was doing in this place. She responded by saying that she was actually a trained nurse and not a medical volunteer and that she had even studied at medical college for a short time.

Before she turned away, he made a note of her name: Ella Neumann. After all, not only was she pretty, she was kind, smart – anyone who attended medical school had to be intelligent – and spoke German. In short, he couldn't relay any sensitive information to the other prisoners.

He was used to the disdain from the Allied military personnel and volunteers, but he was not accustomed to the kindness of Miss Ella Neumann. Of course, he had no business even thinking about a woman in time of war. There were too many jobs, and too many things to remember for each persona he had.

His true identity was that of Garrett Smith, Allied Canadian intelligence officer. Although he was born

Gerhard Schmidt in Dusseldorf, Germany, in 1894, he and his family moved to Kingston, Ontario, Canada, in 1896, when he was only two years old. In trying to create a more Canadian-sounding name, his parents changed their surname to Smith. He remembered nothing of Germany until his family visited Dusseldorf five years ago. His parents had actually considered moving back to Germany.

As a political science major, Garrett understood all too well that if they moved back to Germany, he would be conscripted. Thankfully, by the end of that summer, his parents decided to return to Canada, and Garrett finished his last year at Queens College in Kingston.

In May of 1914, he graduated Queens with a political science degree and a minor in German. By mid-August, the Great War had begun. Garrett had planned on continuing his education at Queens. But at that time, all patriotic Canadians enlisted. So he did too. Besides, he wanted to fight for his country.

During officers' training, the head of command learned that Garrett spoke fluent and flawless German. They offered him an opportunity to be an Allied spy in the German forces. He said yes without thinking it through. That's the way he did most things. Reflecting made no sense to him. If he was meant to die that way, then he was meant to die.

He may be German by birth, but he was Canadian through and through. He played ice hockey, ice-skated on the Rideau Canal every year in Ottawa with his kid brother Hank and enjoyed Shepherd's Pie and tourtière. Canada was – and is – where his loyalty would remain.

Garrett was given all the appropriate materials and sent to Britain by ship. Then he was brought to Germany under cover of darkness to the dormitory of the Duisburg-Essen

University near Dusseldorf. The Allies had registered him as a post-graduate law student, having supposedly received his undergrad from the same university.

His German alter-ego's story was the same as his own, except he was given a German passport and papers that stated he had lived in Germany – rather than Canada – for the past twenty years.

After he arrived in Germany, he made many friends. The Allies told him that there were only two people who knew his true identity: Surgeon-Lieutenant Collins of the American Army stationed here at the compound at Le Tréport and Major Peter Winslow in Soissons, his Canadian contact. Since the war had just begun, Garrett had attended the Duisburg-Essen University until he was conscripted and that happened the following spring. By that point, he had made many friends in Germany and was already thinking in German. He took basic training there, then he was assigned the rank of Major because of his university degree.

After a year in Germany, he spoke and thought in German all the time. He became so comfortable in his alter ego, that days would go by without him thinking of Canada or his family back there.

Admittedly, Garrett didn't expect to last this long during the war. He figured that he would eventually be discovered, hung or shot. Nearly four years later, he was still alive. And the Allies were making great strides against the Axis nations, especially since the Americans joined the war effort.

The stationary hospital here at Le Tréport was more like a hotel than a hospital, and security was minimal. Major Peter Winslow, his contact at the field hospital in Vauxbuin near Soissons, had been correct last week when he told him that the accommodations here were superior to the field hospital in Vauxbuin near Soissons.

Of course, those amenities meant nothing to him because, in about ten hours, he would make his escape. He needed to get back to work. He would return to his original German battalion before sunset the next day.

Chapter Three
Escape

It was 0200 and darkness enveloped the POW tent. It was time for his escape. Although his superior, Lieutenant Collins, had recommended that he wait an additional few days, Garrett couldn't wait any longer. He'd rather be in the field than wasting his time reading week-old newspapers. He sat up and checked his front pocket to make sure the necessary items were there.

A guard was always stationed at the front door of the POW barrack, under an electric lamp. The back door had a loud, metal bell that rang whenever anyone opened the door, which was always kept locked. Garrett had already removed the bell earlier when the pretty nurse, Miss Neumann, stepped out the back door to speak to somebody.   His plan was to slip out after using the lavatory, then head to the area behind the American dining hut because the exit there was rarely monitored.

Miss Ella Neumann was also quite observant, so he did not make a move until she was involved with treating a soldier.

Once she turned her back to him, he made up his cot with pillows underneath the blanket to simulate someone sleeping. He stepped toward the lavatory and she turned her head.

The nurse spoke German, so Garrett said to her in German, "Just using the privy, Miss."

She nodded.

The entrance to the indoor facilities was conveniently located at the rear of the barrack. He put his hand on the doorknob and turned it to open the door. Ella Neumann stared at him, then brought her attention to the patient in front of her. As quickly and as quietly as he could, he unlatched the lock on the back door and stepped inside the lavatory. He figured he would make use of the facilities while he was there. Once finished, he turned the knob slowly and swung open the lavatory door. He took one quick scan of the room. The nurse still with her back to him, leaned over a soldier on a cot. Her curly blond hair draped her back below the headscarf.

He inched toward the back door, slid it open gently, then slipped silently out of the barrack, confident that the nurse wouldn't see or hear him. He tiptoed along the long tent to stay out of the light. He couldn't see them, but one guard was stationed at the entrance of the POW barrack and two were on duty at the front of the hospital complex, so he'd have to stay in the shadows and escape through the dining hut on the other side of the complex.

***

Ella's head snapped up. She turned and saw that the lavatory door was still open. *Where is Major Schmidt?*

She stood up, then took a mental attendance of the cots. The occupied cots all seemed occupied, even the major's cot. But that couldn't be. He couldn't have finished his business in the lavatory and covered himself up and gone to sleep that quickly.

No, someone *had* left the barrack. A feeling of dread came over her, and she raced across the barrack to the back door. It was unlocked!

Ella pulled the door open and stepped outside into the

warm spring evening air. She could just make out the silhouette of a soldier creeping along the side wall of the barrack.

"Excuse me, sir?" she called out loudly in German, her heart pounding. "Please step into the light."

The man didn't move.

"Sir? Step into the light so I may see who you are."

Still no movement.

Instead of waiting for him to comply, she straightened, took a breath and walked toward him. It was only then that the man inched forward, a shadow on his face. She couldn't see him, but she was certain it was Major Schmidt.

"I...uh...was...uh... just stepping out for some... fresh air," he said in German, waving his hands.

Ella scowled. *I don't think so.* She continued in German, "I don't remember you asking for permission to come outside. You asked permission to go to the lavatory."

"Oh, I'm sorry."

"Well, I will remain with you while you finish breathing in the fresh air, then I will accompany you back into the barrack. You must understand that I will be reprimanded if I allow a POW soldier to be outside." She paused. "Why did you unlock the door?"

The man smiled, but it seemed forced. Then he replied, this time in English, "I don't remember unlocking it. I suppose I should just go with you back inside. I've had enough fresh air for the evening."

"I should say so."

This man had no German accent when he spoke English and certainly no English accent when he spoke German.

His smooth voice sounded kind and gentle. Ah, yes, she remembered him: this was the man with the large birthmark on his shoulder.

***

Now what? He could run, but she would call the nearby guards to apprehend him. He tried to appear nonchalant, but he balled his fists in frustration. He'd have to wait until a future date and try again.

Garrett considered reaching for the gun tucked in his waistband. Collins had given it to him. He could use it to threaten her so he could escape.

The girl folded her arms across her chest, smiled, her foot tapping, waiting for him to comply. She was brave, but he was twice her size and could easily overpower her. He could knock her unconscious, leave her in the shadows and take off. She'd be reprimanded for letting him escape. She—the sweetest and most intelligent girl he'd ever met – would get in trouble because of him.

Strange that he'd never considered the repercussions for the person in charge when he had escaped the other POW camp. Truthfully, he'd never cared. Even so, this camp was one with little security. He should have known that this nurse would be so aware of everything going on around her.

He would have to contact Collins in the morning to inform him that it was not going to be as easy to escape this time. Until then, he would bide his time and do nothing.

***

Nearing the door to the barrack, Ella motioned for the German officer to enter before her. As she did so, she noticed that the bell hadn't dinged when they entered. She scanned the area near the door and found the large bell sitting on the floor a few feet away. Did the major also remove the bell? She picked it up and stared at the top of the door, knowing that she would not be able to reach the nail that usually held the bell. She glanced at the major.

"Would you like me to put that back for you?" Again, the man spoke in English with no obvious accent.

"Yes, please," she responded in English, "especially if you were the one who removed it."

"Why would I remove the bell?" he asked.

Her eyes narrowed in suspicion. But she stepped aside and allowed him to attach the bell to the door. Then she closed the door and locked it. For extra security, she placed a chair in front of the door.

The major walked to his cot and removed the pillows from his cot. She returned to the prisoner whose wounds she was dressing and finished, all the while keeping her eye on the major. Could he really have tried to escape? There was something about him – she couldn't quite put her finger on what – but she wouldn't report him to Sr. Nora. She could imagine what would've happened had he been successful. After all, Sr. Nora was just waiting for Ella to do something that warranted discipline.

Chapter Four
A Life Saved

Her co-worker, Clara, relieved her at 0600, and Ella quietly instructed her to keep a close eye on Major Schmidt. The girl didn't question her but said that she would.

Ella returned to her dormitory to sleep.

She woke mid-afternoon, took a quick shower, and prepared herself for her next shift at the POW barrack.

First, she made a brief detour to the post office, hopeful that she'd find a letter from one of her family members. The young French man behind the counter held out an envelope for her before she even stepped inside the small building.

"You have a letter, *Mademoiselle*."

"*Merci*." She took the envelope, a smile stretching across her face to see her brother's name on the back of it. She tore it open and could hear Frank's voice as she read.

May 5, 1918

Dear Elle,

I hope this letter finds you well and enjoying your little holiday on the coast of France. Thank you for the postcard. Are you sure there's a war going on there? Le Tréport looks too picturesque to be a military hospital.

You should see Rose just about now. Mama says that she isn't due for another six weeks, but her middle is quite large. Mama and Papa smile all the time. You would think they were having a baby!

I do hope this war doesn't go on too much longer, or I may be conscripted in a year or two. As much as I want to see you, I don't relish the thought of fighting in a war.

Freed and Maire miss you, and you shall be receiving their letters hopefully before the war ends. They keep drawing pictures and adding words to their letters, which by the way, are still sitting on the dining room table.

All kidding aside, I miss you, Elle. Please keep safe over there and come back in one piece. Praying for you.

Your loving brother,

Frank

Frank was the only one in her family to refer to her as Elle, without the "a." Of course, he referred to Rosa as Rose, to Frida and Maria as Freed and Maire. He told her that he preferred to call people by one-syllable names. Everyone, that is, except for their parents, whom he called Mama and Papa, never Ma or Pa.

As much as she enjoyed receiving her family's letters, they sometimes made her heart ache. Ella pressed the letter against her chest, then placed it in her apron pocket. She missed each member of her family, and by the time she returned back home, Frida and Maria would have grown another few inches.

When Ella arrived at the POW barrack, she went to Major Schmidt's cot but found the cot empty and its linens and sheets removed.

Clara was helping one of the men in the far corner of the barrack. Clara was also an American, was shorter than Ella, and wore small, wire-rimmed glasses. The girl enlisted as a volunteer with no medical background. However, Clara was so kind and hardworking that what she lacked in medical background, she gained in bedside manner.

"Clara," she called, as she approached the girl.

Clara turned. "Hello, Ella!" Her high-pitched voice sounded more like a child's than an adult's.

"Where is Major Schmidt?"

"Lieutenant Collins came in and escorted him out of the barrack at 1600."

"I wonder why."

"Not sure. They spoke German on the way out."

"I see." Ella clutched the back of her neck and shook her head. She darted a gaze toward the major's now-empty cot. Certainly the major was not being punished. And if he only stepped out of the barrack without permission, why would there be an issue?

Ella clasped her hands together and avoided eye contact with Clara. Ella was pretty certain that the man was, in fact, trying to escape. It was too much of a coincidence that the bell was missing, the door unlocked, the major needed to use the lavatory. She wanted to believe him *but*....

The pillows left on his bed, then seeing him outside the barrack indicated that he *was* trying to escape. Besides, why would Lieutenant Collins speak to him in German? The major obviously could speak perfect English, and the lieutenant had to know that. "And you're certain that Lieutenant Collins spoke German to the major?"

"Yes, I'm sure." She paused, then giggled. "Did you ever notice..."

"Notice what?"

"How gigantic the lieutenant is."

Ella broke into a smile, despite her concern.

"I mean," Clara said, "the gentleman's head practically touches the top of the door frame."

"You're right, but I've only ever seen him from afar, never close up."

"Well, I feel like I'm standing in a hole when I stand next to him," Clara quipped.

The two girls laughed.

***

It was peculiar how Collins had told him to remain quiet until they were safely in the *camion* and away from the hospital.

That Collins had ushered him out of the back door of the POW barrack was even more peculiar. The man then escorted him through a side door of the British hospital/hotel to the alleyway where a *camion* was parked.

In the *camion*, Garrett opened his mouth to speak to Collins, but the older man held his hand up for Garrett to cease speaking. "And for God's sake, stay down!" He pushed Garrett's head below the dashboard of the *camion*. "I'm trying to get you out of here without anyone seeing you."

Collins drove but said nothing.

Where were they going? He couldn't see much from his cramped position on the passenger side. From the faint smell of manure, whoever had been in this *camion* last had stepped in cow patties.

Why was Collins trying to get him out of here without anyone seeing him? Did the girl report him? Is that what this was about?

Garrett admired Collins, but the older man could be abrupt and caustic at times. He stared at Collins while he drove, waiting for a sign that he might speak. The lieutenant sat ramrod straight, the top of his head brushing the canopy directly above them, his eyes facing ahead, his body an imposing presence even in a *camion*.

As soon as they were a mile or so from the hospital, Collins said in English, "Now, you may speak, Major."

Garrett pulled himself up and straightened on the seat. "I tried to escape last night as scheduled, but the girl on duty was more observant than most girls. My mistake. I was going to try when another nurse was on duty."

Collins sat quietly and did not respond for several long moments. Garrett shifted in his seat and gazed out the window at fields, the green of the grass dulled by the cloudy day. Was he about to be dishonorably discharged? If so, he likely deserved it.

After several long minutes, Collins cleared his throat. "You're lucky, Smith."

"Lucky, sir?"

"Yes."

"Why?"

"Because the nurse prevented you from escaping."

"Why would that make me lucky?"

The man took a long breath and exhaled. He spoke, his voice smooth and deep, his words slow and drawn-out, as if he were from the South but without the accent. "This morning, we received intel that the Germans know you are working for us and have issued a reward for your capture. They plan on putting you in front of a firing squad as soon as you are captured."

Garrett's entire body tensed. "H...How? Who? I don't..."

"Someone from the field hospital near Soissons recognized you."

Garrett squeezed his eyes shut, trying to remember anyone who could have recognized him.

"You do understand the implications of that, Smith?"

"Uh, yes, sir, I believe I do, sir."

"That nurse saved your life."

"Yes, sir." He paused. "Now, what?"

"You'll be given another identity. We'll keep you out of the public eye for a month, and then you'll be working back at the stationary hospital as an ambulance driver and stretcher-bearer. We're in dreadfully short supply of those."

"Yes, sir."

Garrett had often enjoyed the cloak and dagger of espionage, but being an ambulance driver would clearly not be the most dangerous mission he would have here in France.

"I don't have your file in front of me. What's your natural hair color?"

"What you see is my natural color, sir. Sandy blond."

"Good, then you will need to have your hair dyed brown and shave off the moustache. We'll get you eyeglasses to complete the disguise."

"Very well. When will I receive my identity?"

Collins pursed his lips. "We've had no time to create your identity. Do you have a name in mind?"

Garrett opened his mouth, then shut it. The name Gary was close to Garrett and his mother's maiden name was Braun. "What about Gary Brown?"

"Fine. Corporal. It's best that you take on the identity of an enlisted man as opposed to an officer."

"Yes, sir. When will I report for duty in Le Tréport?"

"In three weeks, after this whole thing blows over, you'll be picked up and taken to a small town near Le Tréport, Mers-les-Bains. You'll get some training there first as a driver and stretcher-bearer."

"Three weeks? Three weeks of doing nothing? It'll be worse than being in the POW ward. Please, sir, can I not just go back to Le Tréport and work in the kitchen? I'd rather be working than bored out of my mind."

"This will be work, Smith. Besides, you need to keep out of the public eye for a few weeks. In the past week, two agents have gone missing in action. I'd rather have you missing but know where you are."

Collins pulled the *camion* in front of *Église Saint-Sépulcre d'Abbeville*. "You'll be staying with an elderly couple," Collins offered. "They'll help you with your transformation and provide food and lodging. The man should be here to meet you at 1500."

Garrett checked his watch. It was only 1400, so he'd have an hour to wait. The two men got out, shook hands, then Garrett made his way inside the church. He dipped his finger in the holy water font and genuflected before stepping into the back pew. He knelt and recited a quiet prayer of thanksgiving to God that he was still alive.

If someone had told him yesterday that his escape would

have been thwarted by a pretty nurse, and that said escape would've resulted in his life being saved, he wouldn't have believed them.

This new position with less danger meant that he would likely be going home after the war – although he couldn't tell his parents until the war was over. And for the first time since enlisting, he allowed himself to think of the future.

He sat on the pew. Having had no rest since his escape attempt, he could hardly keep his eyes open. He relaxed, his head leaning against the rigid back of the pew.

***

Garrett startled as he felt tapping on his shoulder. He opened his eyes, surprised that he had fallen asleep, and turned. There in front of him stood an elderly man with deep wrinkles and a pronounced scowl that made him immediately straighten.

"Mate, are you the Canadian needing food and shelter?" the man asked in accented English – British? No, perhaps Australian.

"Yes, yes, I am."

The elderly man looked down at his paper. "Lieutenant Collins sent you?"

"Yes, sir."

"The name's Noah, mate."

Garrett stood and shook the man's hand. "Thank you, Noah."

Noah genuflected, then Garrett did the same, and they headed outside. Garrett squinted as he stepped outside. The sun was now shining brightly.

"Nothing but small talk on the way to the house.

Understood?"

"Yes, Noah."

After a moment of silence, Garrett asked, "Noah, how long have you been living in France?"

"Since I met and married my wife fifty-two years ago. Madelaine will have a very tasty dinner ready for us when we return."

With war-time rationing, the meal would not likely include meat. But Garrett didn't care. The elderly man walked briskly, and Garrett almost had to sprint to keep up with the man.

Abbeville was not unlike most small war-torn towns. But like Le Tréport, it was surprisingly free of damage. Stone streets made Garrett's feet throb, but the picturesque sights of an old clock tower and Victorian rowhomes distracted him from the pain. They stepped onto a small wooden bridge that took them over a wide stream. He gazed downward. The water was calm, and a few large fish were visible in the water.

Would anyone else be there at Noah's home? "Do you have any children?"

"Four. All adults. Two girls, two boys. One of our boys died a year ago. Blasted war. We have fifteen grandchildren."

Garrett nodded. "I'm sorry to hear about your son."

"Yes, me too. Me too."

They approached a rowhouse, and Noah opened the door and motioned for Garrett to enter. Two carved armchairs faced a couch in a small, but cozy, living room. A savory aroma wafted in from the kitchen.

An elderly woman with dark brown hair pulled back in a

bun emerged from the kitchen and wiped her hands on her apron. *"Bienvenue!"*

Garrett didn't know as much French as he should, but her cheery tone and expression made him feel welcome. *"Merci, Madame."*

"Noah tells me you are Canadian?" she said in English.

"Yes, ma'am."

"What is your name?"

"Gary Brown, Corporal Gary Brown of the Canadian Army." His new name didn't yet flow smoothly from his mouth.

"Well, it's nice to meet you, Corporal Brown. I've got supper ready. Please do come into the kitchen and sit down."

The kitchen was tiny, with room only for an icebox, a small stove and a table and two chairs. He sat in one of them, then stood up. "Where will you sit, ma'am?"

"Don't worry about me. I'll eat when you men are done. Please sit."

"Thank you."

She served hot pea soup and hard bread. It was the most delicious meatless soup he'd had in many months.

"This is tasty. Thank you, ma'am."

"You're welcome, Corporal. It's good to have one of the Allies stay with us."

"Thank you."

As much as Garrett didn't like idle time, he predicted he would enjoy being here in Abbeville. It was simple and comfortable and a welcome change of pace.

Over the next few weeks, Garrett stayed out of the public

eye, rarely going outside at all. He wrote up his own alter-ego's story and memorized it. Madelaine had helped him dye his hair brown.

After two weeks, confident that he had learned everything, Garrett informed Noah he was ready to go.

"I don't think so, mate. We were told you needed to be here for three weeks minimum."

Garrett lowered his head. He was anxious to move on with his new position, but Garrett also respected Noah and would go along with whatever the older man asked.

"But I'll tell you what. Maybe you can come to Mass with us next Sunday, and we'll see how it goes."

"Mass?"

"Yes, Mass. Is your new identity Catholic?"

"I...uh...."

"If you can't answer that, then you're not ready."

During his last week with them, he read whatever books he found on the elderly couple's bookcase in the evening. He didn't usually read for pleasure, so it took a bit of time to become accustomed to it. One book in particular, *A Treasury of War Poetry*, piqued his interest. He'd read through the entire anthology in one sitting, then returned to the book and memorized his favorites. The poem entitled, "Prayer of a Soldier in France," by Sergeant Joyce Kilmer moved him the most. He never considered that a soldier's suffering was akin to Christ's suffering on the Cross: "My shoulders ache beneath my pack, (lie easier, Cross, upon His back)." The poem read more like a prayer.

I march with feet that burn and smart
(Tread, Holy Feet, upon my heart).

Men shout at me who may not speak
(They scourged Thy back and smote Thy cheek).
I may not lift a hand to clear
My eyes of salty drops that sear.
(Then shall my fickle soul forget
Thy Agony of Bloody Sweat?)
My rifle hand is stiff and numb
(From Thy pierced palm red rivers come).
Lord, Thou didst suffer more for me
Than all the hosts of land and sea.
So let me render back again
This millionth of Thy gift.

Garrett even took out their Bible and read a few passages. Was "Gary Brown" Catholic? Well, he assumed both his alter-egos were also Catholic.

So why *had* he stopped going to Mass when he was in college? Garrett shook his head. Because his parents weren't there to remind him or tell him to go. He remembered missing one Sunday, then all the days became one like the other. The next time he attended Mass was at Christmas with his family. He understood that he couldn't go up for Communion since he was not in the state of grace, but he went anyway because he didn't want his folks to know he was no longer going to Mass. Afterwards, he felt guilty for doing so. But not guilty enough to make him go to Confession and return to attending Mass.

Why? Because the sacraments seemed unimportant. His college life was busy with studying and enjoyable activities.

Each day crawled by. Noah, Madelaine, and Garrett relaxed in the couple's living room. Garrett squinted as he read from the book of poetry. He had read that poem by Kilmer over and over again until he had memorized it. But he was tired of reading and wanted to go outside and breathe in the fresh air. He clapped the book closed.

Noah turned to Garrett. "Look, son, many men during time of war don't get the break from war you're getting. Perhaps you should look at this time as a gift instead of a curse."

Garrett nodded, but Noah was right. Each successive day seemed to take longer than the previous day, but he tried to be thankful for the break.

Sunday finally arrived. He accompanied Noah and Madelaine to Mass at the nearby *église*. Once inside the church, he was astonished that he hadn't forgotten the Latin, although he struggled to understand the priest's homily in French.

When the elderly couple processed up to the communion rail to receive the Holy Eucharist, a melancholic mood engulfed him. He couldn't kneel beside them. Oh, he probably could receive – no one would know – except he would know, and that somehow bothered him, made him feel sad, maybe even ashamed because of the last time he had received unworthily. But now? He *wanted* to receive the Eucharist. He made a promise to himself to go to Confession as soon as he could.

When they returned home from Mass, Garrett peered at his reflection in the mirror. With the darker hair, the absence of a moustache, and the rimmed glasses, no one would recognize his former German officer persona. If he had been conscripted into the Canadian Army, he would've been an officer because he had a university education.

On the drive home, Garrett tried to think about his three identities – perhaps he should call them layers. Noah had asked him if this identity (Gary Brown) was Catholic. Yes, he was Catholic. In fact, all three identities were Catholic, even his German identity. But he never attended Mass in Germany nor here in France.

He tilted his head and stared. Who *was* he? Spiritually, he *was* a Catholic, just not a very good one.

And he hadn't been Garrett Smith for many years, at least not when he was with his German battalion. He was surprised at how easy it had been for him to blend in and start thinking like a German officer.

Now he wasn't even a German officer or an Allied officer. He identified as this other person, Gary Brown.

Regardless of his identity, Garrett realized that he had never felt that kind of spiritual longing for the Holy Eucharist the entire time he had been over here in Europe.

He spent the past few weeks becoming accustomed to his new routine of shaving every day and touching up his blond hair. After Madelaine showed him what to do the first time, he insisted on doing it himself every few days.

The day he left, Garrett stood at the elderly couple's door. His heart tugged. This couple had become very dear to him. Madelaine fed him, taught him how to dye his hair and gave him a warm bed. He could never truly repay this couple, but he would think of them and pray for them.

Noah held out a book. Garrett recognized it as *A Treasure of War Poetry* and smiled.

"Madelaine and I think you should have this, mate. Thank you for serving the Allies."

"Thank *you*, Noah." He hugged Madelaine, who had tears in her eyes. "And to you as well...for everything."

Garrett arrived at the basilica to wait for the *camion* to take him to Le Tréport. He waited outside the church for a few moments, then decided to go inside and pray.

It wasn't that he didn't believe in God – he did. In the past two years, whenever he had been injured or in danger, he always prayed to God. And he always felt like God had answered his prayers – in English or German – especially when he heard that he would have faced a firing squad had he escaped and returned to his German battalion. Collins had told him it would be best to wait a day or so before he tried to escape. So why did he not listen to him? He should have faced a firing squad.

Why *had* his life been spared? Not just then, but the four or five times he had been in danger of being killed or discovered.

He genuflected and entered the pew, pulling down the kneeler so he could kneel. He made the Sign of the Cross.

To his right, he heard tapping on the floor and looked up to see a woman coming out of the confessional. Before he knew it, he was inside the confessional and the priest opened the screen to hear his confession. His English and German were impeccable, but his French was only passable.

He did his best to indicate how long it had been since he had been to Confession and slowly, but surely, unburdened his soul.

Back in the pew, he recited his penance: one Our Father, one Hail Mary, and one Glory Be. Every day since he had joined the Allies, his soul had carried the weight of the war, the burden of his position. But now his soul felt lighter, calmer and more at peace. Christ had carried the weight of the sins of mankind. Garrett could certainly give the weight of the war to Him. Whatever happened, would happen. It had taken the example of a devout, elderly couple to make him realize that this respite from action had been a great gift to him.

Dear God, I have been lazy, impatient, and self-centered. I'll do my best to attend Mass when I can over here. Please keep me safe until the war is over so I can see my parents and brother again.

Chapter Five
Overqualified

Ella was in the POW barrack changing a soldier's dressing when her co-worker and friend, Clara, told her of an escape attempt by a POW. It brought to mind the German officer's escape attempt a month ago, and she wondered what sort of punishment he had received. She felt sorry and recited a prayer for him that whatever discipline he had received was not too harsh.

She had pestered Sr. Nora – on a weekly basis – to assign her to assist the surgeons in the operating theater. But Sr. Nora always insisted that she do ward work, which meant changing dressings and giving hypodermics or holding basins in front of vomiting soldiers.

Not that she thought those duties were below her; she had so much more knowledge than what she was being used for. The American medical volunteers, who had little to no training, were perfectly suited to that work.

Oma's saying, *Nichts ist jemals so hoffnungslos, wie es scheint (Nothing is ever as hopeless as it seems)* made her smile. Her precious Oma, her mother's mother, had come with her parents to America. Despite having passed away when Ella was only ten, her legacy of overwhelming optimism caused her to remember that a glass was half-full and not half-empty.

Sighing, she made her way to the dormitory barrack.

Perhaps she would make time to say some prayers as she passed the chapel. In the field hospitals and on the battlefields, she found few opportunities to attend Holy Mass. Fortunately, the military chaplain held weekly Mass here.

Behind her, Clara called her name. Ella turned.

"I never thought I'd catch up to you. You're quite a fast walker!" Clara held out an envelope to her. "It's a telegram. It's from your father!"

*What would Papa be...*Ella took hold of the envelope and ripped it open.

Western Union Telegram
Received at Le Tréport, France
June 12, 1918
To: Miss Ella Neumann
Your sister, Rosa, has delivered safely a baby boy weighing 6 lbs, 12 oz. Her son will be christened this weekend as Rudolph John.
Fondly,
Papa

"I'm an aunt! I have a nephew!" She hugged Clara, and the two girls jumped happily.

This was one of those times that she regretted being away from her family. When she eventually saw and met her new nephew, he would likely be a toddler. She shook her head and put aside the thought. *I'll ask Rosa to take him to the photographer and send me a picture of him.*

Clara bid her farewell. Ella continued walking. She would definitely stop at the chapel to pray in thanksgiving for little Rudolph's safe delivery.

She had just stepped inside the chapel when a loud siren rang out. She held her hands over her ears. The alarm was coming from behind her. She turned and raced back the way she had come. The main building screeched an alarm signaling that all trained staff were to report to the main building.

Even though Ella was a trained nurse, Sr. Nora had thus far not allowed her to work in that capacity. She hesitated, watching two nurses and three doctors racing to the main building. One of the doctors was tall and broad-shouldered with graying temples – oh, it was Lieutenant Collins. Even from her vantage point, she could see the doctor was well over six-and-a-half feet tall. She thought about Clara's previous comment and smiled.

Surely, there must be more than two trained nurses and three doctors? Perhaps they were far away and would take a few minutes to arrive. Even so, large numbers of casualties meant trained medical staff would be needed. Drawing close to the main building, she didn't wait to ask anyone. Instead, she walked briskly across the dirt path, weaving in and out of numerous women now crowding the path.

As she opened the door, someone tapped her shoulder. Ella turned to find her elderly supervisor.

"My dear, you may go elsewhere. This is for experienced staff only."

"But I *am* experienced, Sister. I worked as a surgical nurse for a year before enlisting."

"Surgical experience in a civilian hospital means nothing. Move along."

"And I attended a half-year of medical school."

Sr. Nora scowled and pushed Ella aside as other medical personnel clambered through the doorway.

With her mouth gaping open, Ella could only watch as Sr. Nora pranced into the main building, a sneer stretching across her wrinkly face.

Chapter Six
New Identity

The *camion* took Garrett to *Mers-les-Bains*, but as he passed the stationary hospital, he wondered if the nurse who had prevented him from escaping – and saved his life – was still there. Miss Ella Neumann. Hard to forget her lovely face and demeanour. Hopefully, she would be at the POW ward at some point in the next few weeks. Perhaps he would see her there. Then again, maybe she would recognize him. He shook his head. He was disguised and in a completely different setting.

***

Ella indulged in the shower longer than she should have. Few girls used the shower tent at two in the morning. And the water was deliciously warm. She had just finished her shift, and her uniform and apron were covered in foul-smelling bodily fluids from several soldiers in the influenza barrack. Every part of her body reeked. As she washed her hair, she recalled her conversation with Sr. Nora.

"Please, Sister, assign me anywhere but the POW barrack. I'm a trained surgical nurse. I've even attended medical college for a semester. I can assist in the operating theater."

The elderly woman had pursed her lips and squinted her eyes. "Yes, I think you're due for a change. You're now assigned to the influenza barrack."

Anyone could hold a cold compress on a soldier's forehead. *Why does that woman hate me?*

She tried to set aside her personal feelings. Her years of experience at the Pennsylvania Hospital made her more capable than most, but she could be of use in so many other settings. And, after a day in the influenza ward, she pined for the POW ward. At least there she could do more. And it was closer. The influenza barrack was on the opposite side of the camp. It took her nearly fifteen minutes on work-weary feet to make it back to the American nurses' dorm.

Turning off the shower, she put her robe on and stepped into her slippers on the floor outside the stall. She made her way to the dressing screen where she had left her nightgown and changed. The biggest perk of her sleeping quarters was that it was next door (three steps from door to door) to the nurses' shower tent.

As she drifted off to sleep, she decided that she would be polite and kind to Sr. Nora and do her best with whatever job she was given.

***

Garrett drove the ambulance up to the main building at Le Tréport. After spending two weeks in training to be an ambulance driver and stretcher-bearer in nearby *Mers-les-Bains*, this would be his first day reporting for duty as Corporal Gary Brown. He wouldn't be a medic, per se, but he was trained to place tourniquets on bleeding men.

For the past ten days, he had been itching to get working again, but the locals training him decided he needed a holiday, so they spent time on the beach after training each day.

He parked, then made his way to Collins' office. Garrett opened the door. Collins' secretary looked up.

"Is Lieutenant Collins here? I'm reporting for duty."

"He's across the hall at Sr. Nora's office; she's the nursing supervisor."

"Thank you." He nodded.

He crossed the hall and paused at the first door. A brass nameplate on the door showed him he'd found the right office: Sr. Nora Brennan, Nursing Supervisor.

The door hung open a bit and voices traveled to him.

"There's no way I will assign that girl to any surgical duties." The woman's voice, which he assumed was Sr. Nora's, sounded exceptionally curt.

"But she comes with surgical training. We could use her in the OR." It was Collins' deep voice.

"She comes with civilian training, not military training."

"Sister, I don't know what you're talking about."

"Besides, I've heard her speak German to the prisoners of war. She has a German name and speaks the language. There's no telling where her priorities are."

"Miss Neumann speaks German, Sister?"

"She most certainly does. Now, do you understand why I don't trust her? I'd keep an eye on her, sir, if I were you."

For a minute or so, Collins made no response. Then he said, "You may keep her in one of the low-level positions for now. But if we need her in OR, you will assign her there. Do I make myself clear?"

Garrett turned and made his way back to Collins' office door. Ella Neumann was the reason that Garrett was still alive. She spoke German – and extremely well – but he understood the bias against anyone with a German name, especially one who spoke German fluently.

Collins exited the office and strode toward him, so

Garrett put out his hand to greet him. "Corporal Gary Brown, ambulance driver, reporting for duty, sir."

Without looking at him or accepting his hand, Collins said, "Do you have papers, Corporal?"

"Yes, I do. If we could just step into your office."

Collins finally made eye contact. He squinted and drew in a breath. "Well, it's good to see you."

Garrett followed Collins past the secretary and into Collins' private office.

Collins held out his hand to shake Garrett's. "I almost didn't recognize you, Corporal. That's good. Hopefully, no one else will."

Chapter Seven
More Than a Nurse

Ella stopped by the chapel barrack on her way to report for duty at the POW tent. For the past few weeks, she recited a daily offering and a short prayer to the Blessed Mother. She prayed for her safety here in France and for her family and for her new nephew. And if she was going to be kind and polite to Sr. Nora, she needed help from supernatural sources and so prayed to St. Gertrude and the Blessed Virgin to intercede for her in that regard.

Of course, Ella hadn't seen Sr. Nora all week. The last time she saw her, the elderly supervisor said she would be assigned to the POW barrack until further notice.

Thankfully, Sr. Gladdie had been in charge for the past week. It made Ella's week, because Sr. Gladdie was the happiest, jolliest person in the whole hospital. Despite the images that they all saw every day, this small middle-aged woman with salt and pepper hair wore a constant smile and always spoke in a kind, gentle voice.

Every evening after her shift, Ella returned to her cot and read through the medical textbooks she had brought with her. Two of the books, *Gray's Anatomy* and *Surgical Sutures,* she had bought brand new from a first-year medical student who had quit the program. Of course, they were now dog-eared and marked-up because of the number of times she had read and studied them. Ella also managed to find a revised edition of *Treating War*

Wounds by Jean Baptiste Abadie.

If Ella was going to spend the bulk of her work duties with less-than-challenging responsibilities, then she would spend most of her free time studying.

But on this bright and sunny day, she wanted to spend some time at the chapel before reporting to the POW barrack. Entering the dimly lit chapel, she dipped her finger in the holy water font and made the Sign of the Cross. She genuflected and knelt.

She checked her timepiece, blessed herself, then stood. After genuflecting, she exited the chapel. The sun shone brightly, and Ella couldn't help but be in a positive mood. That is, until she saw Sr. Nora waiting for her at the entrance to the POW tent.

Ella groaned inwardly. The woman always stared at Ella as if Ella had a distasteful mole on the tip of her nose. What could *she* want?

"Lieutenant Collins would like to speak with you."

"You mean the commander of this hospital?"

"Yes. Go on. Don't keep him waiting." She pointed Ella toward the main building.

As Ella marched ahead, she heard the elderly woman's labored breathing and footsteps behind her. Sr. Nora said not to keep the lieutenant waiting, so Ella sprinted, hoping to outrun the woman.

Ella stepped onto the porch, then into the foyer of the main building. She glanced back at Sr. Nora, who had stopped before the porch and stood catching her breath. The woman frowned and pointed to the left. Ella approached a door. In the middle of it hung a brass plate with Lieutenant Collins' name on it. Before she put her hand out to knock, she glanced back at Sr. Nora, whose smug smirk now made Ella think that she had done something wrong and perhaps she was about to be disciplined for it.

She knocked and opened the door. The middle-aged secretary raised her eyebrows and peered at Ella over her glasses. "Yes?"

"I'm here to see Lieutenant Collins."

"Miss Ella Neumann?"

"Yes, ma'am."

"The lieutenant is waiting for you."

"Thank you."

She knocked on the inner office door and heard, "Come in please."

Suddenly, her heart raced. What if she really *had* done something wrong, or Sr. Nora said she did something wrong? She willed her heart to stop beating so quickly, gripped the knob, and opened the door. The lieutenant was just walking out from behind his desk.

Ella stepped back as the man approached her. Lord, this man was tall and broad-shouldered. His head nearly brushed the ceiling. At five feet, two inches, Ella had to lift her chin to look at him.

"Miss Neumann, I presume?"

"Yes, sir."

He held out a chair for her near the desk, then when she sat down, he lowered himself to his chair. He cleared his throat. "You must be wondering why I have asked to see you."

"Yes, sir."

"Well, Sr. Nora..."

Oh, no. Sr. Nora's been talking to him.

The stick phone on his desk rang. "Excuse me." Picking up the receiver and putting it to his ear, he said, "Collins here." Then he mostly listened as someone on the other end spoke. He finally hung the receiver back on its hook.

"Now, where were we?"

"Uh..." Ella didn't want to say Sr. Nora's name.

"Oh, yes. Sr. Nora tells me that you speak fluent German."

Ella sighed, relieved. It didn't sound like she was in trouble. "I do, yes. My parents were born in Hamburg but have called Philadelphia home for the past 25 years."

"And you grew up speaking both German and English?"

"Yes. I also speak a bit of French, enough to get by anyway."

"Marvelous."

Why is he is interested in what languages I speak?

"Well, I wanted to ask you another question, Miss Neumann. Sr. Nora also tells me that you have been on duty in the POW barrack, is that correct?"

"It is. But..."

"But?"

"I'm actually a trained surgical nurse, and I have a half-year of training at medical school."

"Yes, I understand."

"You do?"

"Yes. But that's not why I called you here."

Shoulders slumping, Ella pursed her lips. Of course, that wasn't why he called her here. She shook her head.

"You are already working in the POW barrack and you speak German, so I was hoping you might consider..."

"Yes?"

"Perhaps listening to the enemy soldiers' conversations and reporting back to me what they say."

Ella drew in a breath, her hand to her mouth. Then, scowling, she asked, "You want me to spy on the prisoners of war by listening to their conversations and telling you about them?"

"Correct."

"I...I don't know what to say. I...."

"Then say yes."

"I mean, I do know what to say. The answer is no. I will not do that."

"Surely, you're not working for the Germans?" He lifted his chin and scowled.

"Of course not, sir. There's only one side I'm working for and that's the human race. I am helping soldiers. I won't eavesdrop on their conversations."

"It would be helpful to the Allies if you did so."

She lowered her head and reflected. Some of these men could be distant relatives or cousins. No, she couldn't do this. She could not betray them. "The answer is no, sir. That is, if I have a choice."

"You do."

"Then no, I cannot help in this way. Of course, one way I could help is in surgery, assisting doctors in the operating theater."

Collins sat back in his chair, his gaze fixed on Ella. He said nothing for a moment or two, just stared at her. No smile, no frown. From the graying at his temples, Ella surmised he was maybe 45-50 years old, but remained a ruggedly handsome man. Then he stood up. "Very well, Miss Neumann. I respect your desire to help all the soldiers."

"Is there any way for me to be transferred to the surgical ward?"

"I'll see what I can do, but Sr. Nora usually handles that."

"Yes, of course, she does," she said, her shoulders slumped, and her stomach clenched. *Will I never have an opportunity to use my skills?*

The commander walked to the door, opened it for her, then closed it behind her. Ella nodded to the secretary and hurried out to the foyer. Sr. Nora was standing by the door to her office. She approached Ella.

"What did he want?"

"You don't know?"

"No."

Ella tried not to smirk. The lieutenant had been willing to entrust her with a job that he wouldn't have asked anyone else to do, not even Sr. Nora. The elderly woman scowled, and she tapped her foot while she waited. Finally, Ella said, "Then perhaps I should keep that information between the lieutenant and myself."

Frowning, Sr. Nora huffed and returned to her office.

Chapter Eight
Working Together

Garrett had been on base for two weeks but had been driving the ambulance truck constantly to outlying areas and to clearing stations to pick up wounded. As Gary Brown, he had only seen Miss Neumann once in passing, but he was careful not to let his gaze linger too long lest she suspect he had any familiarity with her. From her perspective, they had never met.

Today, Collins told him he could listen in on conversations in the prisoner-of-war unit, professional eavesdropping, as they say. Collins informed him that one of the nurses who worked in the POW unit spoke fluent German but had turned down the offer to professionally eavesdrop. From the conversation between the nursing supervisor and Collins that he overheard a few weeks ago, he was certain that was Ella. She had spoken to him in flawless German the night he tried to escape and seemed sympathetic to the German soldiers. However, if she was working with the enemy, she would have let him escape. No, she was loyal to the Allies, he would stake his life on that. Like him, she must've had parents born in Germany. There were many Americans, Brits, and Canadians like that, born in an Allied country but with close relatives in the Axis countries.

Collins indicated that his "official job" at the POW barrack that day would be to clean up the ward and that he was to report for duty at 1400.

Would *she* be there? Just the thought of it lifted his spirits. On his way back to his dorm barrack, he whistled and a bird flying above him seemed to answer him. It was going to be a good day.

***

The sun shone in a cloudless sky, the color an intense cerulean. It was neither warm nor cool, "just right," as they say. Ella proceeded to the POW ward that afternoon. She was scheduled to begin at 1400.

She suspected that her decision not to eavesdrop on the German soldiers might have cost her any chance of working in the operating theater. But if that was the case, so be it. When she had decided to take the position of nurse at an Allied hospital in France, she had also made up her mind to treat and care for men, regardless of which side they were on. It was the only way she could live with herself.

She passed her friend Ann Fremont, an American medical volunteer and fellow passenger on the boat over here. Ann had just been transferred to Le Tréport, and Ella couldn't be happier to have a friendly and familiar face nearby.

She entered the ward. The stench of vomit and urine filled the air, and she held the back of her hand up against her nose to stifle the odor.

Nadine Benoit, a French medical volunteer, was sitting on a chair by the medical cart, reading.

To the left and right of her, German soldiers moaned. Vomit and urine dotted the floor near the cots.

"Mademoiselle Benoit?"

"*Oui*?" she asked, without looking up over her book.

"Why is this ward such a mess?"

"Because I don't have time to clean ta men who killed my family."

Ella clenched her jaw and began to pace. Finally, she made eye contact with the girl. "Nadine, these men did not kill your family."

"How am I to know wedder zay deed or not?"

"They deserve to be treated with dignity and respect."

"So...report me."

All Ella could do was sigh.

The girl closed her book and stood up. She sauntered across the ward to the door and left, the door slamming behind her.

Scanning the room, Ella had no idea where to start. At that moment, an Allied soldier came in the back door. He glanced up, took off his cap, and strolled towards her. He looked to be in his twenties, had brown hair and wire-rimmed glasses. His shoulder insignia indicated that he was a Canadian corporal.

"Excuse me, ma'am?"

Ella wondered whether he also spoke French, since many Canadians did. "Yes?"

"My...uh... name is Corporal Gary Brown. I was assigned to clean the barrack this afternoon."

Did Ella hear correctly? This man was like an answer to a prayer.

"I'm quite happy to see you, Corporal. As you can see, the previous attendant in charge decided she wasn't going to clean up after the enemy soldiers. Now that we are getting more French volunteers, I suppose we should expect that."

"I suppose so." The man avoided eye contact.

"I'm not sure where to begin. I'll start with the soldier closest to the door and work back. Perhaps you can clean the floor of the soldier across from him and work your way back as well."

"Sounds like a good plan."

Ella went to work immediately. She spotted no bodily fluids under the first soldier's cot, but from the smell of the blankets, the poor man had wet himself. She tossed aside the blankets and the man moaned. "Shhh," she whispered. Then in German, she said, "It'll be fine. I'm here to clean you up."

She took a fresh clean cloth from the nearby cart, then removed his clothes, careful not to pull off any of his freshly burned skin on both legs. She shook her head. How excruciating it must've been for him to lie in the urine-soaked clothes and bedding. Ella took a pitcher of water from the nearby cart and gently cleaned the man. When she finished, she called for the corporal.

"Yes?"

"Come here, please."

"How can I help?"

"I'll need for you to lift this man up so that I can slide clean bedding underneath him."

***

Garrett nodded and eased the now unclothed soldier toward himself. The man moaned at the movement, but Miss Neumann worked quickly, stripping away the linen and washing the cot underneath.

He cleared his throat awkwardly. He held firm and when she finished putting clean linen down, she indicated for him to lay the man back down, which he did carefully.

Without glancing up at him, she said, "Thank you," and proceeded to dress the man in clean clothes. Garrett stepped back, mesmerized. The girl seemed driven to make sure this man was comfortable, despite the fact that he was an enemy soldier. Her expression of kindness when the man cried out in pain and her use of the German phrase *Ich bin hier, alles ist gut* (I'm here, it's fine) to calm him down – well, it was one of the most compassionate acts he'd seen over here.

When she noticed him staring at her, he backed away and returned to the task of cleaning the floor.

***

Ella managed to wash three cots before she came to a conscious soldier. In German, he said, "I'm clean enough. Help the other men instead."

She replied, *"Danke."* She was touched by the man's unselfishness. In German, she said, "I will make sure you get clean linen when I'm finished."

He offered her a slight smile and nod.

The soldiers in the next two cots needed minimal attention, but the cot against the far wall was probably the worst mess yet. Ella glanced at the man's face and lifted the covers. His eyes were fixed, and he wasn't moving. She felt for a pulse. This poor fellow had died in his own filth. She clenched her fists, then recited a prayer for his soul.

The way a few of the French volunteers treated these men made her angry. For the first time since Ella had arrived in France, she was happy to be taking care of these men.

Chapter Nine
Becoming Acquainted

After the cots and men were cleaned and bedding replaced, Ella finally had a chance to sit down for a moment. Corporal Brown, who had excused himself to use the privy, appeared again and approached her as she sat.

"Miss..."

"Neumann."

The man smiled. He had a beautiful smile with straight, white teeth, unusual for any man these days unless they came from wealth. And the deepest blue eyes that shone through wire-rimmed spectacles. As he spoke, though, she tilted her head. His voice seemed strangely familiar.

"I wanted to tell you that I admire the compassion you've shown towards enemy soldiers."

"It's my duty to treat each soldier with the respect they deserve, Corporal. I did not enlist to fight or to win a war. I came here to care for soldiers."

"Yes." He paused. "You seem to know more than the average medical assistant, though."

"I'm a trained surgical nurse."

"Why are you doing the job of a medical volunteer?"

"Because my nursing supervisor doesn't trust me. She thinks I'm a German spy – which is ridiculous – because of my name and the fact that I speak German."

"Oh." The corporal looked away and seemed to be hiding

a smile. "Perhaps this is where you are meant to be, then."

"Perhaps."

The door squeaked open and slammed shut. She glanced up to see her friend Ann strolling towards Ella and Corporal Brown.

Ann smiled and she touched Ella's arm. "Um..."

"Yes, Ann?"

"Well, um, Sr. Nora wishes to see you immediately. She told me to take over for you."

"Very well."

Corporal Brown stood up. "Well, I believe my job here is finished. Good day, Miss Neumann. Good day, Miss..."

"Fremont."

"Miss Fremont."

"Good day," the two girls replied.

Corporal Brown left as the two girls began to chat.

"What does 'Her Royal Highness' want, Ann?"

"Not sure, but it might have something to do with the influx of wounded coming. This may be your chance to work in the operating theater."

"I hope so, but I won't get my hopes up." She turned to leave. "Goodbye, Ann. Take care of them."

"I will."

Chapter Ten
Saving the Enemy

Ella stopped at the latrine before heading to the main building and the nursing supervisor's office. She had no idea when she might have a break, so she took the opportunity.

When she emerged, numerous ambulances and *camions* waited at the front of the main building in the distance. As she got closer, Corporal Brown entered one of the ambulances, and he sped off.

Inside the building, groaning patients lay on stretchers and cots along the walls of the corridors and in every nook and cranny. Doctors barked orders, and nurses scurried this way and that.

Sr. Nora's office was empty, so Ella waited, her foot tapping. Nurses, medical volunteers, and attendants hovered over patients.

"Miss Neumann?!"

Ella turned toward the screeching sound of her name. The nursing supervisor scowled. "Quickly, girl!"

She dodged gurneys, carts, and other medical personnel to arrive at the right-hand corridor near the operating theaters.

"Yes, ma'am?"

"We've just received an influx of wounded from

surrounding clearing stations. The field hospitals are overcrowded. Fighting nearby, so we've had to take them. I'm leaving you in charge of the wounded here in the foyer before they're taken into the OR. Don't do anything; just watch. You think you can handle that?"

Lowering her head, Ella nodded. At least this was something different, so she acquiesced. "But...."

"But what?"

"What if one of these men needs care?"

Sr. Nora shrugged her shoulders. "They've already gone through pre-op. Besides, most of them are enemy soldiers."

Ella tilted her head and stared at Sr. Nora. "What do you mean?"

The elderly woman ignored Ella's question, called three nurses' names and they followed her down the corridor to the operating theaters.

Left in the foyer beside Ella were ten wounded soldiers and two medical volunteers. One of them was Nadine Benoit, who had left the POW ward in a mess.

For two hours, Ella paced the foyer and merely watched. Nadine and her friend carried on a conversation in French.

Gurgling sounds drew her attention to a man on a cot near the doorway. The two French girls did not move, nor did they even pause their conversation.

"Ladies, there is a problem here, come help."

They stood still and shook their heads. "*Officier Allemand.*" *German officer.* Nadine then said in English, "We were ordered by Sr. Nora not ta do anyting."

Ella threw her hands up. How could they be so cruel? Nadine was correct, though. They were told *not* to do anything.

Ella rushed to the man. Blood spurted from his mouth. He was choking. She flung his blanket back to assess the situation. More blood—a shrapnel wound in his chest. Just then his eyes fluttered open, and his gaze found Ella, his look saying she was the answer to his prayers.

She nodded and said in German, "Yes, I will help." Racing toward a cart, she pushed aside instruments until she found a scalpel and a small glass tube. She put on gloves and returned to the German officer.

"I'm sorry, but this is going to hurt," she said in German. Then she moved his shirt out of the way until she could see his Adam's apple and just below it, where she needed to make an incision. She made a half-inch cut, half-inch deep, from the Adam's apple to the cricoid cartilage. She pinched the incision before slipping the glass tube inside. Blood gushed out and he finally took a deep breath.

The man's body relaxed, and he smiled at her. He opened his mouth, presumedly to say, "thank you," but with the tube in his throat, all he could do was mouth what she supposed was *Vielen Dank.*

"*Bitte.*" Ella squeezed the man's hand and remained beside him until he was taken into the operating theater an hour later.

Chapter Eleven
Gratitude

When she reported to the elderly nursing supervisor for duty, she hoped – in her wildest imagination – that the woman might assign her to the OR, but Ella was also a realist.

No one had said anything the previous night about Ella saving the German officer's life. She certainly wasn't going to volunteer the information. Would the two French medical workers report her? Really, what *was* there to report? She saved a man's life. The fact that she disobeyed an order and that he was a German officer might make Sr. Nora angry, but Ella didn't care.

When she arrived at Sr. Nora's office, the woman sat at her desk, reading a paper. Ella cleared her voice.

Sr. Nora looked up over her glasses. "Yes?"

"I'm reporting for duty."

Sister placed the paper down and leaned back in her chair. She stared at Ella, her lips pursed. "I hear you disobeyed an order last evening."

"Oh?"

"The German officer. Did you think we wouldn't see the glass vial stuck in his trachea?"

"He was choking on his own blood. He would've died."

"You disobeyed an order."

"But, Sister –"

The woman waved her hand to stop Ella from speaking. But she continued. "Sister, why would you tell me to do nothing when I have the knowledge to assist in complicated operations?"

"Yes, you saved a man's life. But it seems suspect to me that he also happened to be a German officer."

Ella pursed her lips but remained silent. This woman was really a major thorn in Ella's side.

"You may work at the POW ward again. We're caught up here in the surgical ward."

Ella's spirit and shoulders lowered. "Yes, ma'am."

On the way to the POW ward, she passed by the YMCA/cinema and noted that the film playing this week, *American Aristocracy*, starred Douglas Fairbanks. She had only seen one other of the actor's films. She had taken her three younger siblings one Saturday last year to see *Manhattan Madness*. They had all enjoyed the film, especially Frank, who had decided he would someday move to Arizona and become a cowboy.

An ambulance drove past, and she heard a whistle, then, "Miss Neumann!"

She turned toward the vehicle. Corporal Brown waved to her. She smiled and returned the gesture.

Admittedly, she found the corporal a jovial gentleman, and he *was* handsome. There was also something strangely familiar about him.

She opened then closed the door of the POW barrack and was pleased to see her friend, Ann, who always treated the POWs well.

The barrack smelled cleaner than yesterday, and the floors were almost as spotless as yesterday just after

Corporal Brown had mopped them.

Ann turned and waved for her to approach. "The German officer in the corner," she pointed, "wishes to speak with you. He asked for you by name, Ella. His name is Major Wilhelm von Kirchbach."

"Really?"

"Yes."

Ella smiled, finished her task, then crossed the ward and approached the cot of the German officer. She drew in a breath as she realized that this was the man she had helped in the foyer of the main building.

He no longer had the tube in his throat and his eyes brightened when he saw her. He was a middle-aged man with graying blond hair, clean-shaven, and a ruggedly handsome face.

"*Fraulein*, I vish to zank you for saving my life."

"You speak English?"

"Yes. *Danke tausendmal.*"

"Well, it was my pleasure to be able to help you."

"If you ever need anything, *fraulein,* anything, I promise I vill help you, vutever you need." He first placed his hand on his heart, then he reached for her hand. She took hold of it. He squeezed her hand once. "I hope you call on me someday to help you."

"Really, that's not necessary, sir."

"No, I insist. I owe you my life. Anything you need."

"Thank you, sir."

***

Garrett parked the ambulance behind the main building and went to retrieve the cleaning supplies so he could spend the rest of the evening in the POW ward. Collins told him that there was a high-ranking officer in the ward today.

"Good evening, Miss Neumann," he called from the door to the ward.

"Good evening, Corporal." She had her back to him as she sat at the desk, writing.

"Just came to clean the floors."

She turned to face him. "Thank you, although the floors are still clean from the exceptional job you did yesterday."

"Then I'll just touch them up."

"Thank you." Miss Neumann returned to her writing.

It was a quiet night. Most of the wounded soldiers slept, although the officer in the corner remained awake. Every time Garrett glanced at him, the man stared back. His stares were starting to make Garrett edgy. He couldn't recognize him, could he? He had met this particular German officer several times. He had hoped his brown hair, wire-rimmed glasses and no facial hair was enough to disguise him. Of course, the only attributes he couldn't do anything about were his blue eyes and the big, dark birthmark on his right shoulder. The only time anyone saw the mole was when he was in the showers or if he happened to take his shirt off. Then again, most of his German comrades had never seen his birthmark, only a few who had commented about it in the showers.

Finally, the officer motioned for Garrett to come over. Garrett glanced over his shoulder. Was he speaking to someone else?

Garrett crossed the room and stood at the foot of the man's cot, his chin downward, avoiding eye contact.

"Do you speak German?" the officer asked in German.

"Uh...what are you –"

Behind him, Ella called, "He is asking if you speak German."

"Uh, nope, except for *danke* and *fraulein*." He did his best to sound like a Canadian saying those words and without proper pronunciation.

Garrett raised his head and made eye contact. The officer tilted his head. Was he convinced or did he question the veracity of Garrett's statement?

***

Ella watched as the corporal approached the German officer's cot and spoke to him. She wondered why the prisoner called to him. She inched her way toward the officer's cot, but Gary then turned and strolled toward her.

"Is everything all right?"

"Yes, yes. As you heard, he wanted to know if I spoke German."

"Do you?"

"No. As I said, I can only say a few words, like *fraulein* and *danke*."

She smiled, but the way he said *fraulein* and *danke* sounded so...native and natural to her ears.

Ella escorted him to the back door of the ward.

"You only say those words and yet you say them perfectly."

"Well, since I only know two words, I try to pronounce them the best I can."

There were times when he spoke simply and directly...authentically. But this, for some reason, didn't seem to be one of those occasions. She couldn't explain why, but she didn't believe him. Did this man, in fact, speak German? And if he did, she understood why he would lie to the officer, but to *her*?

Chapter Twelve
Suspicions

Garrett didn't want to lie to Ella, but he couldn't tell her that he spoke German. Most Canadians spoke English, and many spoke French. Very few spoke German. It would be a dead giveaway.

He wanted to know about her, though. And she spoke the language as if born in Germany. "*You* speak German, though," he said.

"I do."

"Where did you learn it?"

"My parents. They were born in Germany. They spoke it when I was growing up in Philadelphia."

"I see."

"They didn't want me to enlist. I told them I would be helping people, not fighting in a war."

"That's good."

***

The door opened and slammed shut. Ella looked up to see Ann arrive to relieve her of duty.

"My shift is over, Corporal."

"May I walk you back to the barracks? It is rather late."

"Yes, if you promise to learn a few more German words from me."

"Very well."

Ella bid goodbye to Ann as she and the corporal left. It was 0200, and the moon shone brightly in the sky.

"Let's start with numbers," she said.

"Numbers?"

"Numbers are the easiest to learn. *Eins* is number one."

"*Eins*," he said. "Seems easy enough."

"Two is *zwei*."

"*Zwei*." He appeared to be taking his time saying each word clearly. But Ella could not rid herself of the feeling this man spoke German.

"*Drei* is three."

The corporal said in a hushed voice, "I... like when there aren't many people around and... it's quiet. It's not often quiet around here."

"Yes, I know." If Ella was going to test him, this was the time.

In German, she asked, "Where were you stationed before?"

"*Ich –*" His mouth fell open, he stopped walking, and he pursed his lips. "I was stationed in..."

"You speak German, Corporal." She crossed her arms in front of her chest and tapped her foot.

His mouth gaped open, and his entire face reddened with a blush. He pulled at his collar but remained silent.

"The way you said those two German words in the barrack back there, they were clear and sounded German."

"I see."

"I don't like to be lied to, Corporal."

"Please... call... me Gary," he stammered.

"I prefer Corporal. We should keep it professional, Corporal."

***

Garrett felt like a fool. He had spent the past three years as a German officer, and no one had discovered he was a spy for the Allies. Within a few weeks of seeing this girl again, he could barely put two words together in a sentence. And now she had figured out that he spoke German.

And he was torn. Could he tell her a partial truth? Collins had already asked her to eavesdrop. Yes, he would tell her that, since it was true.

"My parents were also born in Germany, so it was my first language growing up in Canada. We moved to Canada when I was two years old. The commander asked me to listen in on the German POWs."

"I see." Ella scowled at him without speaking. Then the frown turned to a smile. Her shoulders relaxed, and she leaned in close. "You don't have a problem spying on these men?"

Garrett opened his mouth to speak, then shut it. He spoke quietly. "No, I don't, if it helps to end this war sooner."

"I see." She paused and lowered her head, as if reflecting on his answer, then she smiled. "Well, I suppose we have our German ancestry and language in common then, don't we?" Her grin grew wider.

He returned the gesture, relieved. "Yes, we do." Under the moonlit sky, her face shone like that of an angel's. Her skin was pale and smooth.

She walked ahead of him.

He called to her, "Wait."

She slowed her pace and turned around.

He inched close to her and whispered, "I didn't want to admit the truth in there, in case that German officer understood English. None of those soldiers can know that I speak and understand German."

Ella nodded. "So where were you stationed before this?" she asked, her eyebrows lifting.

"Near Soissons, closer to the front."

"It must've been horrible there."

"It was, but you notice the horrors here too. Limbs blown off, atrocities I would never have believed – or even cared about – had I not been there."

"As much as we see here, I'm happy that we're not as close to the fighting."

***

Ella was relieved to hear that the corporal had reason to lie. She stared at his blue eyes.

"Are you on duty tomorrow, Miss Neumann?" he asked. His voice sounded gentle and kind.

"No, thankfully, I'm not. You?"

"Yes, I'll be in the POW ward for the morning."

When they passed by the chapel, Ella made the Sign of the Cross and from the corner of her eye, she saw that the corporal did the same. She stopped and turned toward him. "You're Catholic also?"

"Yes."

"Well, there is a Catholic chapel here on base. When I'm not on duty, I attend Mass on Sunday."

"I'd very much like to attend Mass with you."

Ella didn't know why, but the fact that he was Catholic and desired to attend Mass with her made her trust him more. He was also very well-spoken and obviously well-educated. "You attended college. What did you study?"

"Yes. Political science. I was twenty when I graduated."

"Wait. You were only twenty and you had a degree already?"

"Yes."

"That's remarkable."

"I graduated high school at age sixteen and completed my university undergraduate degree at twenty. I was hoping to go on to complete a Master's and Doctorate, but with the war, that never happened."

"That's still remarkable." Many men seemed threatened by her intelligence, but Ella doubted that this man would feel that way, given his academic achievements.

"I suppose."

"Do you correspond with your parents?"

***

Garrett had already given her too much information about himself. True information. He couldn't correspond with his parents because he was involved in espionage. But he wouldn't elaborate. "Not very often."

"That's too bad. I'm sure they're worried about you."

"I'm sure they are." When Garrett enlisted in the war effort in 1915, he could only tell his parents that they would not likely be hearing from him often, but that he would send messages via other sources to let his family know he was still alive.

They reached the dormitory, so Garrett bid goodbye to Ella. He wanted to kiss her, but that wouldn't be proper. Besides, it was the first time Garrett felt so strongly about a girl. He kept his heart closed from members of the opposite sex for the entire time he was undercover. He enjoyed flirting, but that was where it would have to end.

Ella smiled. "Goodnight. Thank you for walking me."

"*Du bist immer willkommen!*"

(You are always welcome.)

Chapter Thirteen
An Opportunity Presents Itself

Ella woke to the quiet din of women rousing from sleep, and a warm breeze drifting through the dormitory tent. She turned away from the noise and tried to recapture her dream. Sometime later, the scurrying of a rodent under her cot made her sit upright.

The dorm was still dark, but as a girl opened the door near Ella's cot, the sun bathed the area in light. It would be another sunny, hot, sticky summer day, the best kind of day to go to the beach. Thankfully, she wasn't on duty. She just needed to find someone to go with her.

She recalled her conversation with Corporal Brown, and her heart skipped a beat. He was a handsome man and seemed very kind. But he was on duty this morning at the POW ward. Besides, she felt a bit awkward asking him to go to the beach with her in a bathing costume. She didn't know him well enough to appear in such an outfit.

It would be crowded there, but Ella was determined to wear her bathing costume at least once this summer. Perhaps she could cajole a few other girls into coming down to the beach with her.

Ann waved and passed her cot on the way out the door.

"Ann, wait!" Ella sat up and threw the covers off.

She stopped and faced Ella. "Yes?"

"Are you on duty today?" Ella stood, grabbed her robe,

and put it on.

"Unfortunately, I am."   She held the door open for another girl to leave, then smiled sympathetically.

Ella's shoulders sagged. "I was hoping someone would go to the beach with me."

"It'll be a swell day for swimming. I went swimming last week, but the water was frigid."

"I don't mind cold water. Well, have a good day, Ann."

"Thanks for asking. I hope you enjoy your day at the beach."

"I will, I'm sure."

Another girl passed, then another. Ella asked six other girls, four of whom were on duty and two of whom were planning to take the train to Paris for the day.

It wouldn't be the first time Ella visited the beach on her own. But she wouldn't take her bathing costume. Instead, she would pull her skirt up and just dip her feet in the water.

She made her way toward the *funiculaire*. Out of the corner of her eye, she saw someone coming toward her. She turned to find Ann stopping by her side, out of breath. "I was hoping I would reach you before you went to the beach. You weren't in the dormitory."

"What's so urgent?"

"Her Royal Highness requested that I find you and instruct you to come to her office in the main building."

Ella scowled. She was pretty sure she knew what this meant. The nursing supervisor was giving her a shift – and this, her day off. *Darn.*

She accompanied Ann to the main building. Ella stepped

into the foyer and bid her friend goodbye. She knocked on Sr. Nora's door.

"Yes?" she heard.

Ella opened the door. "Good morning, Sister. Ann tells me you wish to see me?"

"Not me, Miss Neumann. Surgeon-Lieutenant Collins wishes to see you."

"He wishes to see *me*?"

"Yes."

"Um...well, all right." She exited the office and crossed the foyer to the commander's office. She knocked and opened the door.

Collins' secretary lifted her chin. "Miss Neumann?"

"Yes. Lieutenant Collins requested to see me?"

"Yes, go ahead in."

Ella opened the door and found the commander at his desk. He glanced at her over his glasses. Wasting no time, he stood up and motioned her to take a seat. She had to lift her chin and look at him because of his tall stature. "Miss Neumann, I'm pleased to see you." When she sat down, he did the same.

"Yes, what can I do for you, sir?"

"I have another – well, opportunity – that I would like you to consider. And if you agree to help us out, I'll make sure that you are assigned to work in the operating theater."

Ella's ears perked up, and she straightened. "You've piqued my interest, sir."

"I was hoping I would." The man paused. "I need a nurse who can speak fluent German."

"If this is about eavesdropping...."

"No, it's not."

"I see."

"There is a small German-held POW camp near the town of Lille at the front. It's not well-known, but it is where the Germans keep American and Canadian officers. It is my understanding that there are ten to fifteen men there. It is also my understanding that they are being treated abhorrently."

Her heart ached at the thought of men being treated so poorly. "Oh, dear."

"I would like you to visit the camp."

"A German camp? A POW camp for Allied officers?"

"Yes."

She paused. Listening to conversation was one thing. Traveling to a German-held POW camp was quite another. "It...sounds dangerous."

"It is, to some extent. But you only need to confirm the numbers they are holding there and how they are treating the prisoners. Also, you'll need to dress and pose as a German nurse, which shouldn't be too difficult for you."

"Sir, I don't know. I don't want to..." She jammed her hands into her apron pockets. If Collins' office was larger, she would've paced while she reflected.

"Look, I understand you don't want to be involved in espionage – and yes, this would be considered espionage – but it is pretty simple. The last time we received a missive from our informant on the inside, they indicated that the camp commander has been asking for another German nurse. I would like to send you there to work for the day. That is all. One day and basically just do a headcount and give some medical attention."

Her heart racing, she stuttered, "With...all due... respect..." She paused and willed her thundering heart to slow its pace. Ella yearned to help—that was the main purpose of her volunteering. "Wait. If you have an informant on the inside, surely you don't need me to count the number of Allied officers there."

"We've lost contact with our informant as of three days ago. We don't know if this person is still alive. Besides, you're a trained nurse, and these men need medical attention anyway." He paused. "Look, there are no sides here. You'll be giving our men medical treatment."

Ella pursed her lips and remained silent.

"Miss Neumann, if you do this, I will order Sr. Nora to assign you to work in the OR when you return."

Ella drew in a breath. This would be her chance to finally work in the OR. "When would I have to go?"

"Tomorrow. It takes about three hours by *camion*, so you'll have to leave early. I've assigned Corporal Brown to go with you as your escort."

Ella straightened, and her heart skipped a beat.

"He will wait for you a half-mile mile from the camp and give you a bicycle to reach the camp, as the roads are rough in that area."

She lowered her head. "I'm afraid I don't know how to ride a bicycle."

"You don't?"

"No, sir."

"Well, I'll ask someone to teach you later today."

"Thank you. Will I need a German nurse's uniform?"

"Already taken care of."

"Thank you."

Collins looked away, then made eye contact with her. "You won't be sorry." He paused. "Be ready at 0500 tomorrow morning at the main building."

"Yes, sir."

"Oh, and wear your hair differently, like perhaps pulled up under the headscarf." He opened a drawer and lifted something out. "These should fit you." He held out a pair of wireframe glasses.

She took them and put them on. They were clear with no prescription.

"Yes, that's perfect," he said. "The glasses do a lot to hide your face. Now, would you be so kind as to tell Corporal Brown I wish to speak to him?"

"Yes, of course." She placed the eyeglasses in her pocket.

"He's in the POW barrack."

"Yes, sir."

Chapter Fourteen
The Bicycle Lesson

She stepped inside the POW ward. Ann was changing a dressing on a German soldier. Corporal Brown sat at the desk on the far side of the ward. She crossed the room and waited, her gaze drifting to the top of his head while he hunched over his work. His shiny dark hair fell in such neat little waves and—oh! Light roots made a line across his scalp. *It's odd that he dyes his hair.*

Ella glanced away, her gaze now falling on a book on the edge of the desk, *A Treasury of War Poetry.*

She tapped him on the shoulder.

He turned and lifted his chin. His eyes widened and he closed the book he was writing in. "Well, this...is a pleasant surprise!" he smiled, but to Ella, it seemed forced. He stood up.

"Good morning. Lieutenant Collins would like to speak to you immediately."

"I thought you were off shift today."

"I am." She paused. "By the way, he wants me to learn how to ride a bicycle."

"Is that so?" he asked, cocking an eyebrow.

She felt her face flush. Was he teasing her? Perhaps she should have explained the reason he needed to teach her. "Yes. Do you know how to ride?"

"I do." He flashed her a wide smile as he leaned against the desk.

Was it getting warm in here? She stared at him. His eyes were such an intense shade of blue, which made her want to keep staring. "Then...perhaps you can...well, you can...teach me." It was more of a statement than a request.

He shifted so his entire body now faced her. "It would be my immense pleasure to do so."

"You'll have to speak to the lieutenant first about that." She pursed her lips, then glanced away. Should she be so forward as to ask him to go to the beach for a stroll?

He continued smiling. Apparently, he enjoyed their banter back and forth, although she was doing most of the bantering. She shifted from one foot to the other. "So, well...uh...after the lesson, will you be available to go for a stroll on the beach later?"

He tilted his head. "I would enjoy that very much. I'll meet you close to the *funiculaire* station at 1430. I'll bring a bicycle with me."

"Wonderful." Ella pointed to the book on the desk, *A Treasury of War Poetry.* "Is that your book?"

His eyes followed her fingers. "Yes, it is. I don't write poetry, but I enjoy reading it. There are some heart-wrenching, beautiful poems in there." He paused. "You may borrow it any time."

"I may just do that." She turned to leave. "Good day."

***

Garrett bid her goodbye and returned to his notations. When Ella tapped him on the shoulder, he had been in the process of transcribing the content of the conversation he had just overheard. Her presence had jolted him because he was concentrating on remembering the conversation.

When he finished writing, he closed the book and straightened. She seemed rather shy as she asked him to teach her how to ride a bicycle. On the one hand, he relished their time together. On the other, he was becoming too relaxed and too familiar with her. She was so kind and lovely. He could even see himself married to her. His *mater* would be happy to hear that he had met a lovely young woman – who happened to be Catholic *and* German – if he made it out of the war alive.

He glanced at the door that Ella had just exited and shook his head. He shouldn't be thinking about the future. For three years, he had stopped picturing himself in the future. He focused only on the present because he didn't know if he would survive the war. Now? Now, he couldn't get her lovely countenance, curly blond hair and bluer-than-blue eyes out of his mind.

Besides, what was wrong with enjoying a simple friendship?

And then for her to stop by and tell him Collins wanted to see him. Why would Collins want him to teach Ella how to ride a bicycle? He suddenly felt dread. Had Collins asked her to go into enemy territory? He hoped not.

When she asked if he would be available for a stroll on the beach, he couldn't say no. He wouldn't go swimming, of course, since he had to keep the mole on his right shoulder hidden. But he was pretty certain she wouldn't be swimming today.

Garrett placed his pencil on the table and exited the POW barrack.

***

Garrett stood outside Collins' office. Should he ask the

lieutenant why Ella needed to learn how to ride a bicycle? The more he thought about it, the heavier his soul felt.

He knocked on the lieutenant's outer door, opened it, and nodded to the secretary. He rapped on Collins' door and heard, "Come in."

Garrett opened the door and went in. "You asked to see me, sir?"

"Yes. I'm sending a nurse to the front, the POW camp near Lille, to get a headcount on the number of officers there and to give medical aid."

Garrett's heart skipped a beat. "And that would be Miss Neumann?"

"Yes."

"Why *her*?"

"She speaks fluent German."

He blew out a sigh. "It sounds dangerous."

"Don't worry. If any enemy soldiers had ever seen her working for us, they won't recognize her. I've instructed her to wear her hair differently under her headscarf. I also gave her a pair of eyeglasses. And...that's also why you're going with her – to drive her there and then to watch from a safe distance."

"When does the bicycle riding come in?"

Collins chuckled. "I see you've been talking with Miss Neumann." His eyebrows rose.

"Yes. She doesn't know how to ride."

"You can teach her. She'll like that." Collins smirked. "Every time I mentioned your name, her face brightened."

"Oh?"

"Yes."

"What's the plan, sir?"

"You'll drive her by *camion* to an area about a half-mile away from the POW camp. She'll have to ride by bicycle from there because the roads are bumpy and unpaved."

He didn't like this. He didn't want to put Ella in danger. She had obviously already agreed to this. His shoulders relaxed. "When do we leave?"

"Tomorrow morning at 0500. She'll arrive at the POW camp tomorrow early and spend one day assisting and caring for the men." He stared down at his desk, then looked up at Garrett.

"You'll be waiting for her at the border town of Lille, she'll ride the bike the half-mile to the camp. Then she'll meet you when she's finished at 1600 tomorrow afternoon."

If Garrett and Ella arrived in Lille by 0800 and left at 1600, they would be there for eight hours, too long a time to merely wait for her. "But I won't be waiting all day for her there."

"Correct. You'll be walking to the hill overlooking the POW camp to ensure she's safe."

"Right. Then I'll be returning quickly to our meeting spot at 1600."

Garrett still didn't like this scenario, but it seemed like a good plan and simple enough. Ella would just be there to get a headcount and treat the injured men. "Miss Neumann doesn't know that I've worked as a spy, right?"

"Correct. I only told her the specifics of tomorrow's day." He stood up. "Any questions?"

"No, sir."

"Do you understand everything?"

"Yes, sir."

"Be extra precautious. We've already lost three agents in the past two weeks. I don't want to lose you."

Garrett lowered his head. "Yes, sir."

"One last thing. She's liable to get cold feet. Spend time with her. Keep her occupied, especially on the trip tomorrow."

"Yes, sir."

"Dismissed."

He returned to the POW barrack and mopped the floor. The shorter medical volunteer – Clare? – was on duty.

His soul felt heavy, not for himself, but for Ella. He shook his head. Garrett handed that anxiety over to Christ. If he – and Ella – were being asked to go on some sort of mission, he had to trust that God – and the lieutenant – knew what they were doing.

***

Ella spent the balance of the morning and the first hour or so of the afternoon reading her medical procedures textbook as she normally would. However, she hadn't turned the page in over an hour. She couldn't stop thinking about her trip into enemy territory tomorrow or the stroll on the beach with Gary. While she was nervous about this "mission" that the lieutenant had asked her to be part of, she was also strangely excited about the adventure. She would finally be using her nursing skills to treat injured and suffering men. Besides, she was looking forward to spending three hours with Corporal Brown traveling there and back again.

As the afternoon progressed, it became more humid. A bead of sweat dripped onto the book, so she stopped and wiped her forehead. It seemed like every part of her body was perspiring, so much so that her clothes stuck to her like taffy. She clapped the book shut, then freshened up in the women's shower tent and made her way to the *funiculaire* behind the Trianon Hotel/British base hospital.

As she strolled, she reveled in the scent of summer. A male civilian was mowing the lawn to the right, and to the left, a group of female volunteers were squealing and splashing buckets of water at each other. From these activities, anyone would think that this was just an ordinary day in an ordinary town anywhere in the world. These days came few and far between, but she relished them.

She passed by the Trianon Hotel and marveled at the beauty of the horseshoe-shaped structure. Square upper-floor windows and tall rectangular first-floor windows complemented the clean, light gray bricks. In its previous lifetime, it certainly must've thrived as a first-class hotel.

Near the *funiculaire* station, Ella waited by the peacock statue. It was only 1345, but she was always more comfortable being early than being late. Three American soldiers passed by. One winked at her; the other two tipped their hats. She smiled and nodded at them. She checked her watch: 1410. He was late, but maybe he had been asked to finish cleaning up before he went off duty.

Across the lawn, closer to the hotel, she heard a couple of girls singing "In the Good Ole Summertime." She leaned against the statue and listened. The girls had lovely voices, and she almost left her waiting spot to move closer.

Her thoughts again drifted to the "mission." If this trip

really *was* dangerous, then Collins certainly wouldn't have asked a civilian to do it, right?

"Good afternoon," Gary's voice came from behind her. Pleased that he had arrived, she turned to greet him. He smiled widely. In his hands, he held a circular metal contraption with wheels and curled bars. He removed his hat.

"Well, good afternoon to you," she said, trying to contain her excitement.

"I apologize for my tardiness." He put his cap back on.

"It's fine, really."

"Do you know what this is?" He lifted it up.

"No, although judging from the two wheels, the pedals, and the bars, it looks strangely like a flat bicycle."

"Indeed it is. It's a folding bicycle; it's one that the Germans use." He pulled it apart and set it up on the ground beside Ella, kicking a metal bar with his foot to allow the contraption to stand upright. Now that it was unfolded, it looked like the other bicycles Ella had seen: handlebars with rubber grips, pedals and spoked wheels with tires. A small canvas bag hung from a long bar that ran from just below the seat to just below the handlebars.

Gary shielded his eyes from the sun and peered outward. "That will work as a stopping point." He pointed to a flagpole fifty feet away. He got onto the bicycle and rode to the pole and back again.

Well, that certainly looks easy.

He stopped, his feet on the ground on either side of the bicycle. "It's really a matter of balance and practice. Do you want to try? I'll hold onto it while you get on."

He steadied the bicycle for her as she lifted her skirt a bit and swung her leg over the seat. She sat on the hard seat, her legs dangling.

"The seat's too high," he said. "I'll need to adjust it so your feet can comfortably reach the ground."

"All right." He held the bike by the handlebars with one hand as he helped her to get off the bicycle with the other.

Gary then took a tool from the canvas bag and adjusted the seat so that it would be lower. "There, let's give that a try."

She straddled the seat once again, and this time, her toes were able to touch the grass below her.

"Excellent. That should work. I don't think the seat will go down any further." He paused. "Now, grab the front bars to see if your foot can reach the brake."

Ella placed her hands on the front bars, but she had no idea where the brake was. "Where is the brake?"

"Right here," he pointed to a pedal below her.

She touched it with her foot.

"Good. Now, without my help, try to get off the bike." He stepped away.

Ella tilted to put all her weight on her right foot, lifted her skirt a bit, then swung her leg over the long bar of the bicycle. She released her skirt and allowed it to straighten in front of her.

"Good, good. The next thing you'll need to learn is to try to move along with the bike but without pedaling." He got on and, with his feet, walked the bicycle along the grass. "Want to try that?"

"Yes." She lifted her skirt, then balanced herself on the seat and pushed along the grass with her feet so the bike scooted across the lawn.

"Ella, you're a quick learner."

"Thank you." She hoisted her leg over the bar and smiled at him.

"The only thing left is to learn how to balance." He got onto the bike, scooted without pedaling, then balanced himself before he began using the pedals. He rode a ways before returning to her. "The key is to be comfortable balancing before you try to use the pedals."

"Very well." Getting onto the bike, she scooted and balanced. She tried a few times to use the pedals, but she didn't quite have the knack yet. A few more times, she nearly fell.

Before she knew it, she was pedaling and riding the bicycle. She squealed, then giggled. It felt like she was riding on air. *I can't believe I did it!*

"You're riding! You did it!" he yelled.

She returned to the statue and got off the bike. "I must give credit to my excellent teacher."

"The only thing left is for you to practice."

"May I ride the bicycle back to my barracks? Then I can also practice after our stroll on the beach."

"Of course. Then you can bring it tomorrow so I can place it in the *camion*."

While she rode the bicycle, he strolled beside her to her dorm. She had to focus on keeping her balance, but she was actually starting to have fun and riding ahead of him while he raced to catch up to her. When they reached the dorm, she pressed down on the brake pedal and stopped, then carefully got off the bicycle. They left it by the back of the tent.

Gary held out his arm and she clasped onto it. The two of

them returned to the terrace station to the *funiculaire* train that would take them through the cliff and down to the beach. As they walked, Ella started to think again about the mission to the German-held POW camp. Her heart picked up its pace and she had to will herself to calm down. He stopped; he must've noticed her sudden change because he asked, "Are you all right?"

"Yes, I'm fine. I'm nervous about tomorrow's trip. I was having such fun learning how to ride the bike that I forgot the reason I was learning."

"You'll do well, Ella."

His confidence in her made her feel a bit braver. On the way down in the *funiculaire*, Ella tried to focus on the beauty of the land below. On a sunny day like today, the blue-green water, the beach, the brightly colored shutters and rooftops of the quaint houses, and the crisp cerulean sky took her breath away. "It's such a beautiful view, isn't it?" she said.

"It is indeed. One of the perks of being stationed here."

She wished the tram traveled slower so she could enjoy the view.

***

Garrett waited until they were walking on the beach before he spoke about any detailed information about the "mission" tomorrow. He would make certain that his blond roots would not be noticeable later this evening after he bid farewell to Ella.

Admittedly, he was still irritated that Collins had asked her to do this and more than surprised that she had agreed. Though she *had* said that she joined the war to help soldiers on both sides of the conflict. This was an ideal way to help Allied soldiers in captivity. And now that she knew how to ride a bicycle, he hoped that would give her more confidence.

He offered his arm and she accepted it.

"What do you know about the mission tomorrow?" he asked.

"Lieutenant Collins told me I would be going to a German POW camp to ascertain how many POW officers were there and give medical aid to the men."

"Right."

"He also told me if I agreed to do this, he'd make sure I would be assigned to the operating theatre permanently."

"That's good." He paused. This was all starting to make sense. Ella had agreed because he promised her she'd be assigned to the OR. He sighed but remained silent. He couldn't change anything about the mission. But, he could ask her questions and find out more about her. "Tell me more about your family," he said.

"I have six younger siblings, although two brothers in between Rosa and Frank died in infancy. But there's Rosa, Frank, Frida, and Maria. Rosa is a year younger than me and is the mother of Rudolph, my new nephew. He's only four weeks old. And the next, Frank, is sixteen. My youngest two sisters, Frida and Maria, are twelve and ten." Her voice became high-pitched the more she spoke about her loved ones.

"Sounds like a fine family. I've only got one brother and he's younger."

"Are you close?"

"We used to be closer. When I went to Queens, he and I drifted apart. However, when I return home, I'm going to spend more time with him. He's a fine gentleman."

"What's his name?"

"Hank."

"What will you do after the war?"

He was surprised at how chatty she was.

Seagulls squawked in the distance as he thought about his response to her question. He breathed in deeply of the salty air and studied the stones on the beach. Finally, he said, "I'll probably get a job teaching high school. There's not much I can do with a political science major, but my parents encouraged me to attend college and study a subject I enjoyed."

"Well, you're an excellent teacher. That would be a good choice."

"What do *you* plan to do after the war?"

"Do you really want to know?" She cocked her head and narrowed her eyes.

"Of course, I do. Why wouldn't I want to know?"

"Because most people think it's an unusual choice for a woman."

"Oh?"

"I wish to finish medical school and be a physician, perhaps a surgeon."

He opened his mouth to speak, but nothing came out. Her answer surprised him, but he was impressed, nonetheless.

"I suppose you don't think I should aspire to be a doctor?"

"No, no," he sputtered. "I think it's admirable."

"Really?"

"Yes."

Ella stared at him as they strolled along the beach. He kept looking back at her smiling face. "What?"

"You're certainly not like most people, Corporal Brown."

"I hope that's a good thing."

"It is."

As they walked along the beach, he studied the ground. The sun reflected off a small stone. He released her arm, reached over and picked up a small stone. "Very unique."

"The stone is unique?"

"Yes. Look." He held the stone on his palm. It was tiny oval, pink and gray with flecks of blue.

"It is lovely."

"You must think *I'm* odd."

"Not at all."

"I collect stones from every place I've ever been to. It's an interesting way to remember where I've travelled, and it doesn't cost anything."

"True. And they're small enough to put in your bag."

"Or pocket." He dropped the small pebble into his shirt pocket and held his arm out for her to grasp.

"How do you remember where you've picked them up?"

"I keep them in a small journal that indicates the description, when and where I picked it up."

Ella checked her timepiece and drew in a breath. "Oh dear, we've missed supper in the dining hut."

"Don't worry. There's always something edible left over."

"I'm not worried." She shrugged. Then she smiled, her entire face lighting up.

His heart skipped a beat. How could any girl be so lovely?

They reached the *terrasse* for the *funiculaire*. A tram was waiting so they stepped on to it. She squeezed his arm and he turned. "This is just about the most fun I've had since coming to France."

"If this is the most fun, then we must see about expanding your experiences."

Chapter Fifteen
Mission to the Front

Ella hardly slept. With nerves and second thoughts in the forefront of her mind, she couldn't help but be excited. As she told Gary the previous afternoon, this mission would likely be the most exciting experience she's had while here in France. She prayed that God would watch over her and that she and Gary would return safe and sound tomorrow evening. Ella was itching to tell someone about this "mission," but none of the other medical volunteers or nurses knew anything about it. She had to keep this to herself. Wanting to make sure everything was in order, she had practiced riding the bike behind the barrack last night. After that, she had visited the chapel briefly to pray for God's protection.

It was still dark when she woke. The plans were for her to change into the new uniform in the back of the *camion* once they reached the front close to the City of Lille. The uniform was similar to hers, except the headscarf was slightly different and the under-blouse and skirt were dark gray instead of blue or white. She packed the German nurse's uniform in the cloth bag and put her hair up in a chignon as the lieutenant had requested.

Finally, at 0440, she rode the bicycle to the main building, then waited. She checked the timepiece on her apron. It was now 0443. It had only taken her three minutes to ride the bicycle to the main building. The walk usually took eight to ten minutes. Yes, she rather liked riding a bicycle.

The sun was just peeking above the horizon in the distance.

It was quiet this time of the morning, although a few soldiers or medical personnel nodded or waved as they passed by.

A warm, earthy breeze swept by her. She checked her watch: 0500.

Gary drove up in a *camion* at preciously 0501 hours.

***

Garrett bid Ella good morning and took the bicycle from her, folded it and put it in the back of the *camion*. He then assisted her into the front passenger seat. Collins had made sure that the back of the *camion* had medical supplies because if they were stopped along the way by the Allies, the story was that he was delivering these items to a field hospital near the border.

The *camion* had no windows in the front, and other than the roof, the front seat was open to the elements. So as he began to drive faster, the wind blew around everything. Ella held her hands to the back of her head, presumedly to keep the bun in place. "Sorry about that," he said.

"It's all right." She took a scarf from her bag and tied it around her head.

She was quiet for the first hour or so. Was she second-guessing this decision to go undercover as a German nurse at the German POW camp? He wished she would talk. The next two hours would drag if she remained silent. But he didn't want to engage her in conversation unless she said something first.

As they drove through rural France, Garrett was struck by the beauty of the countryside with its fields of poppies and purple, yellow, and white wildflowers scattered throughout the region. Even the scent wafting by him seemed stronger than the faint traces of horse and cow manure.

After another half-hour, just as Garrett was opening his mouth to say something about the beautiful landscape, Ella began to talk and didn't stop for the rest of the trip. He was glad, though, because it meant that she felt comfortable with him – and was working through her nerves. And...he learned a lot about her.

A few times, the distant sound of shells and bombs could be heard, but Garrett knew this part of France well enough to steer clear of military action.

***

Although Ella remained quiet at the beginning of the drive to Lille, she now recited her alter-ego's backstory to make sure she had it memorized correctly. She was a German nurse who had been previously working in another POW camp in Germany. She was born in Frankfurt, was the same age as her real identity, had the same first name, but her last name for this mission was Müller. She would be caring for the POW soldiers for the day and then take her leave.

According to Collins, the men hadn't had medical assistance in weeks.

They approached a rich forest with pine trees, then he weaved and swerved to stay at the edge of the forest.

"We're close to Lille."

Ella's heart began to race. They'd come that close to the drop-off point already? She checked her watch. It was only 0730. She needed to be at the POW camp by 0800, so there was ample time to prepare.

"I'm going to take you a bit closer, so you won't have to ride the bike for more than a half-mile."

"Thank you."

***

Gary stopped the *camion* and pulled over to the side of the road before reaching Lille. Lille was still on the German side of the front. From what Garrett understood – and hoped – the Allies would be pushing the front line to the Belgian border within days. There generally wasn't much military action in this area, but the Allies had already pushed the front back in the southernmost sections of France. It was only a matter of time before Lille was liberated.

He helped Ella out of the truck, then assisted her into the back of the *camion* where she changed into the German nurse's uniform. Garrett stepped aside to give her privacy while he set up the bicycle.

"I'm ready," she called and picked up her medical bag of supplies.

Gary came to the back of the *camion* and gasped. "You look different!"

"That's the plan. Do you think anyone will recognize me?"

"Not if they only spent a short time with you, no."

"Good." She straightened the glasses on her face and smoothed out the apron and skirt.

He assisted her down off the *camion* and escorted her to the bicycle. "Now, follow this dirt road, and you'll pass a forest to your left. The front is immediately after the trees.

The field hospital is about a hundred feet from there." He paused and glanced at his watch. "We're about twenty minutes early so please take your time. There might be a guard or two at the front, but that's unlikely. And, remember, even though this area is occupied by the Germans, the citizens here won't take too kindly to any German."

"Yes, of course."

"There looks to be a bit of a steep hill at first so you may want to walk the bike until you get on even ground."

"All right."

***

Ella attached her medical bag to the back of the bike, then waved. "Well, I'm...off," she said in a jovial tone. Her hands were shaking, but she didn't want Gary to know how nervous she was.

"Goodbye," he said. "I'll be right here waiting for you when you return at 1600."

"Yes."

She turned to walk her bicycle. He called to her. "Wait."

Garrett ran to the other side of the bike and faced her. "I'll be praying for you, Ella." He leaned close and whispered, "You will do fine. See you at 1600."

She nodded, took the bike by the handlebars and walked it up the hill of the dirt road. When she made it to level ground, she got on the bike and pedaled.

The sun now shone brightly in the morning sky. She rode the bike and stared at the surroundings. After all, he had told her to take her time. A glint of something on the dirt road caught her eye. She stopped to get a better look. It was a shiny, blue-green stone with pink specks. She got off the bicycle and crouched to retrieve it. After tucking it into her pocket, she got back onto the bike and continued down the desolate, winding dirt road.

The forest came up more quickly than she thought it would, and she rode the bike up to the camp before she could think about backing out.

A German soldier approached her and held his hand up. "*Halt. Ihre Papiere.*" *Halt. Your papers.*

She parked the bicycle and lifted her medical bag off the back of it. Her hands were shaking. Faking a peaceful demeanor, she straightened and handed him the papers for her alter-ego, and he waved her inside the complex. "*Dieser Weg.*" *That way.*

That was almost too easy.

Barbed wire surrounded the camp. There was a stone cottage to her right and a new barn to her left. She followed the pathway to the cottage. Outside, a sign read, "*Kommandant Major Wilhelm von Kirchbach.*" She drew in a breath. Von Kirchbach was the German officer she saved from choking in the foyer of the main building at Le Tréport. Had he escaped? What if he recognized her? She shook her head. She couldn't worry about that at present. At least she was – somewhat – disguised. Ella straightened and opened the door.

A woman sat at a desk and looked up. She was middle-aged, with dark hair pulled back. Ella spoke.

"*Guten Morgen. Ich heiße Fräulein Müller. Ich bin hier, um die Gefangenen medizinisch zu behandeln.*" (*Good morning. I'm Miss Müller. I'm here to give medical attention to the prisoners.*)

"*Guten Morgen, Fräulein Müller. Ich bin Frau Hoffmann. Komm hier entlang.*" (*Good morning, Miss*

Müller. I'm Mrs. Hoffman. Come this way.)

When the woman stood, Ella noticed that she was quite thin, almost emaciated. Of course, most people were skinny during war. She felt sorry for the poor lady, who probably hadn't had a hearty meal in years.

In German, the woman continued, "You'll be treating American and Canadian officers being held here. They haven't had medical treatment in weeks. Don't try to save them. Just make their suffering less painful."

She tilted her head. In German, Ella asked, "I'm not trying to save these men's lives?"

"No."

"Very well." Whether or not she was a German or Allied nurse, she would be disregarding that order. She was here to help these men and – yes – to save their lives.

***

Garrett hoped Ella hadn't noticed the extra bicycle he'd stowed for himself in the back of the *camion*. He waited until she had a half-hour start, then he followed the dirt road past the park, positioned himself on the hillside behind the camp and took out his binoculars. She was easy to spot in the white and grey uniform. An older woman in civilian clothes was walking with her.

***

In German, Mrs. Hoffmann asked her if she was all right. She responded in German that she was fine, just a bit lightheaded from the heat.

Every cell in her body urged her to leave. She straightened and asked Mrs. Hoffmann when she would be treating the POW officers.

"*Sofort.*" Her answer indicated that it would be

immediately.

The woman took her behind the cottage to an old barn with holes in the walls. They stepped inside, and they were greeted with the stench of excrement and urine, the human kind, and it was overpowering the animal waste. The woman opened the first stall to reveal six men lying side by side against piles of hay on the ground and all shackled together.

She turned to Mrs. Hoffmann and in German said, "Would it be possible for me to get water to clean these men up? And dry clothes?"

She responded in German. "Water, yes. But there are no dry clothes. Remember, you're not here to save them. And there are four stalls with four to six officers in them, so if you spent all your time in one stall, the other men will get no medical help from you."

Ella nodded. Gary had informed her that until recently, POW officers had been held under pristine conditions with excellent medical care. It was only in the past few weeks, according to Collins, that the Germans started mistreating the officers and housing them like cattle. In fact, animals were housed better than these poor souls.

The officers were also very thin with pale skin and cracked lips. Dehydrated, she suspected. They were lethargic but conscious and each one smiled at her. She couldn't imagine smiling under such circumstances, but perhaps these men hadn't seen a pleasant face in a while.

She spent three hours in that one stall, and there were four more stalls. After cleaning each man as best she could and putting their stench-filled clothing back on and giving whatever medical attention she could to their wounds – most she assumed were from beatings and torturing – she cleaned out the hay of excrement and urine as well as she could.

That anyone could treat another human being like this made Ella sick. What happened to treating prisoners humanely according to the Hague Convention of 1907? She made note of each officer and their condition. Given their condition, she wished she could say a few English words of comfort to them, but that wouldn't be possible. Instead, she whispered in German, hoping that her tone of voice would speak kindness to them.

In the last stall, all the men were unconscious. The four officers didn't even stir. She felt for a pulse in the first man's neck and was happy to find one, but it was weak. After washing him as best she could, she gave him a shot of morphine. She wasn't sure it would do much good, although it would ease his pain.

The next man had a bloody bandage on his arm so she took her scissors to remove it, washed it as best she could and redressed it. She gave him a morphine injection as well as a tetanus shot.

When she reached the last officer, she felt for a pulse, but couldn't find one. *God rest his soul.* A wave of sadness passed through her, but she dared not linger on it. These men had no one else to offer the slightest degree of comfort and medical attention. She needed to keep working.

Why did Mrs. Hoffman not direct her to treat these men first? What if he had passed while she was treating the other men? She clenched her fists. Because she wasn't here to save these men but to "make them comfortable."

Covered in sweat and filth from the past four hours of work, she climbed to her feet and wiped her hands on a towel.

When she finished, she left the barn and reported to Mrs. Hoffmann that she was ready to leave.

In German, the woman said, "Just one moment. Our commander, Major von Kirchbach, has need of some medical assistance."

Ella's heart lurched. She opened her mouth to speak, but she didn't know what to say.

***

Garrett crouched in the shadows of a mature pine tree near the edge of the cliff overlooking the camp. He peered through his binoculars. Ella passed the main building and stopped. The woman he had seen her walking with earlier spoke to her. He couldn't see Ella's expression, but her stiff body posture told him something was wrong.

Chapter Sixteen
A Close Call

Racking her brain for a way to avoid seeing the major again, Ella finally stammered in German, "Of... course. But if it's... not an emergency, may I please use the latrine first?"

The woman escorted her to the latrine tent – and by the grace of God, it was near the exit. Ella went inside the women's section, which was only one cubicle. Should she try to escape out the back of this small tent and through the exit? She couldn't risk being recognized by von Kirchbach. If they were in the same room together, he might recognize her.

Mrs. Hoffmann called to her in German. "The commander had other plans, so he said he would find medical attention in town. You may leave as soon as you are finished."

Ella drew in a breath, then called out, "*Danke.*" She peeked out the tent to see von Kirchbach getting into a motorcar and leaving the premises. Ella blew out a long breath and felt her entire body relaxing. Now, she just needed to exit the compound and get on her bicycle to meet Gary a mile away.

***

Garrett watched through his binoculars. Ella emerged from the tent and strolled to the exit.

He got on his bicycle and pedaled as fast as he could back to the meeting point near Lille.

***

Ella bid goodbye to the guard and to the POW camp and made her way to the bicycle. She was happy that she had not been discovered but felt badly that she couldn't do more for the poor men in such squalid conditions. The stench from the old barn tickled her nose, likely from the transfer to her clothes. She couldn't wait to get out of them and into her regular uniform. Still carrying her bag, she felt a hand on her back and turned to see the guard, a tall, muscular man, smiling at her. In other circumstances, she might've found this man attractive, but his leer made her uncomfortable.

She glanced past him to see only the lavatory which hid them from the camp. No one could see what this man was doing.

"*Fraulein?*"

"*Ja?*" she managed to stammer.

The man continued his smirk, then grabbed her arm.

In German, he told her she was beautiful and ran his finger down the side of her face. He took off her glasses. She tensed. All she wanted to do was leave before anyone recognized her.

The rumble of a motorcar drawing near broke the quiet. The vehicle pulled up beside them. "What is going on here?" a man asked in German, his voice rough and demanding.

The guard backed away and muttered something.

In German, she heard, "Are you all right, fraulein?"

The voice was unmistakable. It was von Kirchbach. "*Ja, Dankeschön,*" she answered, turning her face away from him and avoiding eye contact.

Von Kirchbach ordered the guard to focus on his duties and to leave the young woman alone.

She snatched the glasses out of the guard's hand, picked up her medical bag and got onto her bicycle. The major's motorcar idled but didn't move. Her heart still racing, she pedaled as fast as her legs could. Behind her, she heard the motorcar drive away. She pedaled so quickly that she had almost made it to their meeting point, a half-mile away, within minutes.

***

Garrett checked the time. 1610. The sun felt warm on his face as he leaned against the *camion* and waited. He had already stowed his folding bicycle in the back.

He stared at the entrance to the dirt road. He heard her voice before he saw her. She was speeding down the hill and screaming that she couldn't stop. She pressed on the brake but since the bicycle was going so fast, she skidded just before she made it to the bottom of the hill and Garrett.

He raced to her and picked her up and helped to dust off her clothes, which smelled worse than they looked.

"I forgot about the hill, then I forgot about how to brake." She lifted her skirt to reveal a brush burn on the side of her calf.

"Are you all right?"

"I'll live." She paused. Her hands trembled, and she was pale. "But..."

He picked up the bike and folded it. "What happened?"

115

"The guard..." Still shaking, she stuttered her words. "Kind of...well, he... made a pass at me."

"A pass? Oh, Ella."

"Thank God that the commander of the unit, Major von Kirchbach, drove by and stopped him before he went further."

"Yes, thank God." He paused. "You're all right?"

"I'm fine. I kept my face away because I treated von Kirchbach a few months ago in the POW barrack. I didn't want him to recognize me."

"That's right. Quick thinking." Garrett clenched his fists. He should have stayed at his post to watch what had transpired. His impatience had gotten the better of him again. He shook his head.

Garrett placed the folding bicycle into the back of the *camion*.

When she began to describe the filthy conditions in which the men were housed, she stopped and burst into tears. Garrett did the only thing he could under the circumstances. He pulled her to an embrace. Her clothes reeked of human and animal excrement.

After she changed into her American nursing uniform in the back of the *camion*, they got into the truck, and Garrett drove away. She was at first understandably quiet, her head lowered, sniffling into her handkerchief, her shoulders drooping. The built-up tension of the mission, the guard making a pass at her, the poor conditions of the men at the camp, must've weighed heavy on her. He tried to coax more information from her, but she only answered in one or two words.

After an hour, she straightened and spoke with a tone of cheerfulness. "Oh, I almost forgot," she said, patting her apron pocket.

"Forgot what?"

"I picked up a pretty stone on my way to the camp."

Garrett's heart skipped a beat. She remembered that he liked stones.

"Oh, darn it. I left it in the apron pocket of the other uniform. I'll show you as soon as we stop."

"I'm sure it's lovely. Thank you for remembering."

"You're welcome. I'll give it to you when we return to Le Tréport." She spoke so quietly that he had to lean towards her to hear over the hum of the vehicle's engine. "I can't believe anyone, even the enemy, would treat human beings like that."

"I agree," he said but didn't elaborate.

"And the filth on the men's clothes and in the stalls was horrendous. I would never treat any animal the way they're treating those prisoners."

Garrett released a long breath. He had been relatively lucky not to have to endure that kind of treatment when he was a prisoner, and he felt bad for those men.

However, he was happy that Ella was chatty again.

***

Back at Le Tréport, Garrett drove the *camion* behind the main building so they could report to Collins and let him know how everything went.

Ella seemed more herself, but she fidgeted in her seat in the *camion* the last hour of the trip. As he assisted her out of the truck, her hands were trembling. *This has been difficult for her*, he thought.

It was one thing for Garrett to go on secret missions. He

had been trained for that. It was quite another for an untrained civilian to do that. She would most certainly have trouble sleeping tonight, despite the long day they shared.

"Wait! Can you open the back of the *camion*? I'd like to get the stone I picked up for you."

"Of course."

He opened the back, and she went in. After a minute, she came out. She held a stone in the palm of her hand. He took it, then assisted her down.

Garrett then took a closer look at the stone; it was a pale blue-green with pink speckles. "This is beautiful. Again, thank you." He stuck it in his pocket.

They went into Collins' outer office, but his secretary was not there. He knocked on Collins' door and heard, "Come in." Collins stood as they entered, then sat down.

The two then explained everything that happened, the atrocious conditions and the soldier she found dead. Ella didn't leave out the part about the guard making a pass at her and von Kirchbach driving by. Collins listened attentively, nodding every few seconds. When she finished, Collins stood up.

"Excellent work, Miss Neumann. Would you please step outside in the hallway while I speak to Corporal Brown privately?"

She tilted her head and scowled. Garrett wondered whether she was going to disobey the order. Instead, she exhaled and complied.

"It's going to be a beautiful, warm evening," Collins said, after Ella left the office.

"Yes...and?"

"And I'd like you to bunk outside her dormitory, so you'll be close in case she has nightmares or screams out. We don't want her roommates to know where she's been."

"Yes, sir. I understand."

He left the office and met with Ella in the foyer. "Why all the secrecy?" she asked.

Not wanting to disturb her with the details, he said, "It was an unrelated matter." He escorted her back to her sleeping quarters. To find out where her cot was, he asked, "Are you close to the front door of the dormitory?"

"Why, yes, I am. Why do you ask?"

"I was just worried that perhaps your roommates might keep you awake opening and closing the door."

"I'm used it to by now. And they're pretty considerate so they usually open and close it quietly."

"That's good."

"Goodnight, Ella." He kissed the top of her head. "It was quite the day, wasn't it?"

She nodded.

When she went inside the tent, he peeked to see exactly where her cot was. She tossed her bag and her hat onto the third cot from the door. He knew exactly where he would position his cot outside so he could listen for any problems.

Chapter Seventeen
Finally!

Even though she had washed in the German POW camp's latrine and had dressed in a clean uniform, she couldn't rid herself of the stench of blood and excrement. So she slipped out of the tent and took a long shower in the women's bathing tent next door and scrubbed every inch of her body. The abrasion on her lower leg burned, but she made sure it was clean.

Still, Ella could not fall asleep. With thoughts of that guard's hands on her face, her mind would not stop replaying the incident. Her body tensed, and she controlled her urge to punch her pillow – and perhaps that guard and Mrs. Hoffman – when she thought of those poor Allied officers being held in such atrocious conditions.

The fact that Major von Kirchbach had stopped his autocar and had reprimanded the guard made her thankful that he prevented the guard from getting too familiar with her. She was relieved he didn't appear to recognize her.

She eventually fell asleep for what seemed like mere minutes before the shriek of the sirens awakened her.

Ella gasped in terror and gripped her sheets. Voices surrounded her. And shuffling. Groaning...Ella sat up, the image of a wounded soldier moving through her mind. So frail, so miserable...

"What time is it?" a woman said.

A woman? Ella shook her head, rousing herself more fully. She was in her sleeping quarters—not the enemy POW camp.

The siren continued to blare, announcing the arrival of more wounded.

She dressed quickly and presented herself to Sr. Nora.

Sr. Nora scowled as Ella stepped into her office. Ella approached the woman.

"I have no idea why Lieutenant Collins is doing this, but..." – the woman glared at Ella – "you're being assigned here in the surgical unit, in the operating theater." Her lips pursed like she had a bad taste in her mouth.

Ella sucked in a breath and suppressed a smile. Collins had kept his end of the bargain. She would finally have an opportunity to put her skills to use in the surgical unit. Not nervous in the least, she put on a clean apron and joined the two surgeons and four other nurses in OR One. Then she donned gloves and a surgical mask.

Dr. Nigel Bennett, a white-haired, British surgeon, said tersely, "If you're supposed to be working in this OR, get over here stat!"

"Yes, sir," Ella responded. Even with the surgical mask on, the man's eyes frowned. Of course, if Ella had operated on so many men with horrible and debilitating injuries, she might be frowning too.

The other surgeon spoke. "I need dat," he pointed to an instrument. When no one listened to him, he barked, "I need dat now, *s'il vous plait*." Ella's heart pounded. Was she expected to give it to him?

One of the nurses swiped it from the tray and handed it to him. Another nurse administered anesthesia.

The head nurse, a middle-aged American who introduced herself as Nurse Rachel, approached Ella. "You'll be assisting Dr. Dubois."

Ella nodded and proceeded to stand beside Dr. Dubois. It was only then that she caught sight of the unconscious soldier on the table. The wound on his face was so bad, it appeared he had no left cheek. And he had an abdominal wound as well.

"These are the instruments Dr. Dubois will be using," Nurse Rachel said. "You have a few moments to familiarize yourself with them."

Once she reviewed the instruments, she stood beside Dr. Dubois. Dr. Bennett had just made an incision on the patient's face. Dr. Dubois began cleaning the abdominal wound.

Ella watched both aspects of the operation with interest. Even though she had not used her surgical skills in months, she was able to find and give Dr. Dubois the instruments he asked for. She was glad she had been assigned to the younger doctor because Dr. Bennett was calling out for instruments with names she didn't recognize.

After the man's face and abdominal wounds were cleaned and repaired, the room was quickly cleaned, new gloves and face masks for all, then another soldier was brought in. This man had a three-inch wide wound in his abdomen, and his intestines had spilled out onto his belly. Within half-an-hour, that man had been sutured, the room was cleaned again, and they received another soldier.

It went like that for seven hours. Ella was in awe of how efficiently the team worked together. "Come with me," Nurse Rachel said. Ella accompanied her to the sink where the nurse tossed the soiled instruments into a big metal pot. She whispered to Ella, "You're doing a splendid job, nurse. Did you just arrive on base?"

"No, I've been here since the end of March."

"What?" she spat out.

"I was using my skills elsewhere."

"Well, we won't be letting you go now that we have you."

Ella straightened, proud of the work she had done. "Thank you."

"Head wound, chest wound, and gangrene in left leg," shouted a nurse who burst into the room with another patient.

Nurse Rachel leaned in close. "This will likely be a three-hour operation. If you need to use the lavatory or clean up, do so immediately. You'll be otherwise occupied for the next three hours."

"Yes, ma'am." Ella removed her face mask and gloves and rushed out to the washroom. She drank in a cool glass of water. Moans echoed down the hall, presumedly from an injured soldier. She returned, put on a new mask and gloves, stood beside Dr. Dubois, and waited for the operation to begin. The man on the table continued to squirm, but he no longer moaned. While Dr. Bennett worked on the head wound, Dr. Dubois operated on the gaping chest wound. Dr. Dubois said, "Dees man was left too long in de field. Not sure how much we can do with tis much damage."

Dr. Bennett nodded and sighed.

Then the two physicians set to work. Three hours sped by, first by amputating his gangrenous left leg below the knee, then by cleaning and suturing the man's head and chest wounds. Ella had only witnessed one amputation at the Woman's Medical College of Pennsylvania, but Dr. Bennett had obviously done far too many of these procedures because he did so efficiently.

Once the man was stable, he was taken to one of the wards.

The day flew by with Ella cleaning and stitching for two more hours. When they were finally finished, Ella was so fatigued after the past few sleepless nights, that she was sure she would sleep twenty hours straight. But her heart still sang. There was nothing like using her skills in the operating theater.

Chapter Eighteen
Surgical Experience Necessary

Ella had slept from the time she returned from the operating room until 0600. Twelve hours. She hadn't seen Gary all yesterday.

The following morning, she was pleasantly surprised that Dr. Bennett had requested that she work with him again in the OR. Sr. Nora's scowl delivered the news as if she was telling a bad joke.

"He requested *me*?"

"Yes. Now, get going."

"Yes, ma'am."

When she arrived in the OR, she proceeded to the basin, washed up, and donned a clean apron, face mask, and gloves. Drs. Bennett and Dubois stood by the table, presumedly waiting for a soldier to be brought in.

Neither doctor wore a face mask. Dr. Bennett was clearly in his fifties or older, now that she got a closer look at him. But this older man must have been handsome in his youth. His mouth turned up in a smile, but it looked more like a grimace. She smiled in return. Dr. Dubois had a headful of curly dark hair and five o'clock shadow on his face.

A soldier was brought in, and Dr. Bennett asked Ella if she would help him with his face mask. She did so, but she had to get on her tiptoes to do it, as the man was close to six feet tall.

While Dr. Dubois operated on the man's neck wound, Dr. Bennett then began working on the man's gaping wide abdominal wound exposing a small coil of the patient's intestines. "The casualty clearing station did an excellent job removing the dead tissue and leaving the wound open." Before he sutured the small wounds, he irrigated the area and for the next five minutes, Ella's primary job was to fetch hot water from the sink close to the doorway. She didn't mind. At least she was working in the operating theater.

However, as Dr. Bennett began to close the wound in the man's abdomen, Ella straightened. He hadn't yet run the bowel, a method of checking whether there were any other nicks in the colon. He shouldn't be closing the wound before doing that first. She was just about to say something when, before anyone knew what was happening, Dr. Bennett swayed, and his chin dropped to his shoulder. The nurses gasped and exchanged glances.

Ella knelt beside Dr. Bennett, pulling the mask away from his face. "Doctor, are you all right?"

Dr. Bennett could only manage a slight shake of his head.

When Ella pressed her hand against his forehead, she found it burning with fever. "He's got a fever, Dr. Dubois."

"You," he said to one of the nurses in the OR, "go find a stretcher and a couple of bearers to take him to de influenza ward."

"You," he said to Ella, "keep irrigating de wound until I can get dere."

"Yes, sir," she said. "But Dr. Bennett hadn't yet run the bowel to see if there were any other nicks."

"Dr. Bennett did not do dat?"

"No, sir."

"Den just keep irrigating."

"But, sir?" I have one year of surgical nurse training as well as six months of medical school. I know how to run the bowel, then suture this man's wound."

Dr. Dubois' brows lifted, and he peered over his glasses at her and then down at the wound. Through his face mask, he said, "Wait 'til I've finished up wit' dis wound in his neck."

"Yes, sir. But..."

The doctor didn't respond, so Ella began running the bowel and lifting the small section up and over. There was indeed a tiny nick. Suddenly, blood seeped out of that area and a faint smell of human excrement wafted by her nose. "Sir? Doctor?"

Dr. Dubois glanced up. "I told you to wait."

Ella fidgeted as she swayed from side to side. The more blood that trickled out, the less likely this man would live. Just then, one of the small bowel wounds that Dr. Bennett had already sutured burst open and now blood gushed forth. She had no choice. Besides, she had already disobeyed the order and checked the bowel. Perhaps she would never have another opportunity to work in the OR, but this man would die before the doctor could get to him.

Ella's shoulders straightened. Her heart pounded so hard, she thought it might explode. She first put pressure on the already sutured wound. She then asked for irrigation and the nurse got her water from the sink.

Once the larger wound was cleaned, Ella then asked for a needle and sutures. This time, the nurse's eyes widened, but she handed over the needle and sutures. Ella repaired that wound. She then cleaned and sutured the tiny nick.

Ella carefully lifted folds of the bowel to make sure there were no other small tears. Sure enough, she found another tiny tear, which she irrigated then sutured. Finally, when she was certain there were no other nicks, she asked for irrigation to cleanse the area.

By this time, Dr. Dubois had finished and stood beside her. He said nothing, but he was so close, she could feel the warmth of his body.

She paused and waited for him to say something like "Get out of here. You disobeyed orders." But he said nothing.

"Sir," she stammered, "I...there...was..."

"Go ahead, nurse. I had no idea you had dat much surgical experience."

Given the length, width, and depth of the abdominal wound, it seemed like it took a long time to suture the varying layers. She concentrated, remembering what she had learned not only in her first six months of medical school, but during the past two days she had been working in the OR. Only once did Dr. Dubois say anything and that was to tell her to use different sutures for the last layer of skin.

Finally, she finished and lifted her chin to see a group of doctors and nurses watching. *Uh-oh*. Sr. Nora stood among them, arms crossed against her chest. Her lips were pursed together in a frown. Behind her own mask, Ella's mouth fell open. She hoped that she wasn't in trouble. After all, she had – eventually – gotten Dr. Dubois' permission.

Then, a round of applause came from the group of medical personnel. Ella's gaze connected with the nursing supervisor's. The deep scowl on the older woman's face seemed now like a permanent fixture.

"My dear," said Dr. Dubois, "dat was nothing less than magnificent. Excellent job. We may just put you in charge of suturing for da remainder of your stay wit' us."

"Thank you, sir. I would be honored."

"Have you just arrived?"

"No, sir. I've been here since the end of March."

"And where have you been assigned?"

"In the POW ward."

"What?" he practically screamed. "Sister, what is the meaning of dis?"

Sr. Nora sputtered and stammered but couldn't quite get any words out.

For a moment, Ella felt guilty pleasure at the woman's embarrassment. Then she felt sorry for her.

"Sister, you can be sure I will be reporting dis to da commander."

"He knows," she finally spit out.

"Well, he will be hearing from me." Then, turning to Ella, Dr. Dubois said, "Nurse Neumann, I look forward to working with you."

Dr. Dubois clapped his hands. "*Vite, vite.* Everyone, back de your stations. We've got surgeries te perform."

***

After another entire day in the operating theater, Ella felt like she was on the top of the world. As she exited the main building, Gary was leaning against a *camion* and waiting for her.

"Well, hello there," he smiled.

"Hello."

"You didn't see me earlier today, did you?"

"No. Did you see *me*?"

"Yes. When I went into the OR to pick up Dr. Bennett and take him to the influenza ward."

"Oh?"

"You were...uh...busy." Gary ended his sentence with a lilt, as if he was pleased.

She chuckled. "Indeed. Wait till I tell you all about it."

Chapter Nineteen
Blossoms

The two of them stood beside the *camion*. It was still early, only 1700, and Garrett had hoped that she might have dinner with him.

He enjoyed listening to Ella speak in rapid-fire sentences about how she saved a wounded man. Earlier when he had gone into the OR to retrieve the sick doctor, he had briefly glanced at Ella. It hadn't appeared as if she was assisting. A nurse stood beside her and had handed her instruments, indicating that she was actually performing a procedure. It didn't escape his observation that when she was concentrating, she scowled. Sometimes she pursed her lips together, but because of the face mask, he only saw her scowl.

Even several months ago when, as a German POW, he spoke with her, she impressed him as one of the most intelligent people he had ever met. Anyone who wanted to be a doctor *had* to be smart. For being one of the "fairer sex," she could likely win any intellectual competition against any man.

"Dr. Dubois asked me to do all the suturing from now on!" she said, her voice high-pitched, and her hands waving.

"Come," Garrett said, "let's sit over there under the tree." Across the road was a bench in front of an oak tree. He took her by the arm, and the two sat on the bench. "That's the most incredible story I've heard during this horrid war," he said, waiting for her to make eye contact. When she did, her eyes were so bright, and she smiled as wide as her narrow face would allow.

"Yesterday, I worked for a short time as a surgeon."

"I know! I'm very proud of you, Ella."

"I can't wait to write to my family to let them know."

His heart had stopped yesterday when she told him of the German guard making a pass at her. Now, though, as she chattered excitedly about the day's events, his heart leapt with joy. He could not deny his affection for her. He loved everything about her: her eyes, her pretty face, her intelligence, her generosity, her selflessness. Now that he was no longer working in dangerous espionage, he could envision the future and could see himself married to her.

He stood up. "Are you hungry?"

"Not really. I need to rest for a while."

Garrett escorted her to her dorm. "I'm not working this evening. May we have dinner together in the dining hut in a few hours?"

"Yes, that would be lovely."

"Till then."

***

Ella walked on air. First, her successful day in the operating theater, then spending time with Gary...it was all so exciting. Even in the midst of a war, she had so much joy inside her, she thought she would burst. But her bones ached, and her feet felt like they were on fire. She opened the flap to the barrack and found her cot, unlaced her shoes, took off her headscarf and apron, and then lay down.

***

Garrett had controlled his impulse to kiss Ella. He had wanted to. No, he ached to do so. But he did not want to kiss her unless he asked permission, especially since her run-in with the guard yesterday. He would have weeks, if not months, for other opportunities to kiss her.

At 1900, Garrett met Ella in the dining hall. From the bounce in her step, he assumed she had gotten adequate rest. After getting their food – mutton, ribbon potatoes, and string beans – they sat down, and she chattered on and on about her exciting day. She hardly touched her food.

Garrett could easily get drunk with happiness listening to her speak so quickly. Her voice was a delight to his ears.

"And do you know what the Brits are allowing me to do?"

He shook his head.

"They're allowing me to stay overnight in one of the rooms at the Trianon, the British Hospital on the hill." She pointed behind her. "It's a first-class hotel with indoor facilities and even tubs for bathing." She stopped to sip her water. "I can't wait to have a nice, hot bath!"

He tried not to think of her bathing in a tub and changed the subject. "The mutton's quite good. Better eat up."

Ella stared at her food and drew in a breath. "Oh, I nearly forgot. Yes, I shall eat." She stabbed a small piece of mutton with her fork and put it in her mouth.

The murmuring din of the dining tent became background noise as Garrett kept stealing glances in her direction. This would be an opportune time to discover what her intentions were after the war. So, while she ate, he chatted. "When I return home to Canada after the war, I'd like to tell my family about you. Perhaps I can bring you there to meet them. My mother will love you, although she will try to fatten you up."

She stopped chewing and swallowed. "Pray tell, what will you say about me?"

"Only that you are the loveliest, kindest, and smartest person I've ever known."

Her eyes became moist, and she blinked. Had he offended her?

"That..." she started.

He tilted his head and listened.

"... is the sweetest thing anyone's ever said about me."

"It is?" He cocked his eyebrow.

"You think I'm the smartest person you've ever known?"

He pursed his lips to keep from smirking. It didn't appear that she had heard that she was lovely and kind, only the part about being smart. Of course, it was unusual these days for anyone to state in public that a woman was smart, but Garrett firmly believed that although females might not be as strong physically as males, as a whole, members of the fairer sex *were* smarter. And Ella was a notch above most women because she knew so much about so many different things.

"Yes, indeed, Ella."

***

When Gary said her name, he said it with such care, almost with reverence. He was a fine man, one who had listened to her, comforted her, and laughed with her. If he wanted her to meet his parents, Ella was smart enough to know that that could only mean one thing. She believed a person should state exactly what was on his or her mind without prevaricating or beating around the bush.

"So..." – she cleared her throat – "where do you see the both of us in three years' time?"

He straightened and smiled. "What do you mean?"

"When you say I'm one of the most intelligent people you've known, does that mean you have – affection – for me? That you see a future for us?"

He laughed out loud, and it made her smile. "Miss Ella Neumann, you certainly are one of a kind!"

"I should hope so."

"Yes, I have much more than affection for you. But I'd prefer to continue this...uh...dialogue after we finish our supper and I walk you back to the dormitory."

"Of course." She ate more quickly in anticipation of their "continued dialogue."

***

Gary held the door open for her, then took her hand. She relished the feeling of his warm, strong hand in hers.

They walked together in companionable silence. As they approached her barrack, there were no other people around. Ella began to speak. "When..."

He stopped, turned toward her, her hand still in his. She became quiet and tilted her head. He lifted her hand to his lips and kissed her palm.

When he finally brought his intense gaze to hers, she blinked her glistening eyes.

"I love you, Ella. I hope one day you will agree to be my bride."

Her face warmed with a blush. "I love you, Gary. And I hope one day you will ask me to be your bride."

Gary leaned in and placed a simple kiss on her cheek,

then kissed her lightly on the lips.

Her eyes were still closed when he spoke again.

"Goodnight, Ella."

Opening her eyes, she whispered, "Goodnight."

She nearly bounced into the dormitory. But as it was only 2000 hours, there were few, if any, girls in the barrack. Ann was nowhere to be seen. Ella wished she could tell someone, anyone, that a man had just kissed her. But, alas, none of her friends or co-workers were in the tent.

And finally, to be kissed by a man! She shivered. She thanked God that that despicable German guard hadn't gone so far as to kiss her. Thank God for Major von Kirchbach. And thank God for Gary, a kind Canadian who would, she hoped, someday be her husband.

Chapter Twenty
More Promises

By the end of September, the Allied Forces had succeeded in pushing back the front to Belgium. Ella had read in last week's newspaper that the enemy was admitting defeat, and some German troops were already surrendering. From all reports, the war might be over soon.

In the OR every day for the past few weeks, Ella had stitched just about every wound in the first operating theatre. She had become faster and more proficient. Dr. Dubois had offered to teach her some of the more minor injury repairs, so she was also doing those and learning more each day.

On this beautiful autumn day, Ella was stuck in the dining hall, treating minor injuries. They ran out of supplies, so she headed for the officers' barrack where most of the supplies were kept. She opened the door and stopped when she saw Julia Murphy, whom she met on the ship over here to France.

Ann had already shared that Julia had also joined them in Le Tréport, but Ella had not seen her before now.

They embraced.

"Julia! How lovely to see you! Ann told me you were here. And that you're engaged. How splendid for you."

"Ann tells me you have news of your own?"

"Yes, I do. But I don't think the story is over yet. I'll tell you what I can when you are free. It really does seem like the war has turned in favor of the Allies."

Ella thought of Gary and how much she enjoyed spending time with him. But other than seeing him in passing, she hadn't seen him in several days.

"Yes," Julia replied.

"Well, I must get some supplies, but I should be here in Le Tréport for at least a few weeks."

"It looks like I'm going back to Soissons for a short while. So we won't be able to see much of each other. Perhaps when the war is actually over?"

"Oh, yes, of course."

Ella went to the supply closet, took out sheets, blankets, and bandages, then left.

***

Garrett strode toward the dining hut. He had hoped that Ella wouldn't be busy this evening as he wanted to ask her to the cinema. He had already looked for her in the main building, but she wasn't there.

"Gary!" he heard behind him. He turned. Ella was fifty feet away carrying an armful of blankets. He raced towards her.

"Ella!" Just the sight of her made his heart race.

"Hello! It's been too long."

"Yes, I've missed you." He paused and held out his arms. "Please allow me to carry that for you."

She placed the linens in his arms. "Thank you." She stepped back. "I've missed you too."

They strolled together to the dining hut. Ella said, "We

needed linens and blankets, so I had to go to the influenza ward to get the supplies."

"I'm glad I found you."

"Were you looking for me?"

"I was. I was hoping that you might have time to go to the cinema after your shift. I'm free this evening."

Ella stopped and turned toward him. "I'm done at 1900. When does the picture begin?"

"Perfect. The picture starts at 2000 hours."

They continued walking. "What's playing?"

"I believe it's a picture called *Stella Maris* with Mary Pickford."

"Mary Pickford is wonderful. Do you know what it's about?"

"I'm not sure, but I think from reading the poster at the cinema, it might be about a love triangle."

"Sounds interesting. Shall I meet you at the cinema?"

"I can pick you up at the nurses' dorm. It'll be a beautiful evening to walk."

"That sounds fine."

They went inside, and Ella led Garrett to a cabinet, where he placed the blankets. "See you at 1930. Will that give you enough time to freshen up?"

"More than enough time, thank you."

He left the dining hut with more than a bounce in his step, anxious for their time together.

***

After her shift, Ella quickly made her way to the dorm and changed into another skirt and blouse. She draped a sweater over her arm. She had just emerged from the barrack when Gary showed up to take her to the cinema. He looked handsome in his uniform. Ella greeted him. "Hello!"

"Good evening." He held out his arm and she took hold of it. He gazed upward at the clear sky before dusk. "When the film is over, we'll be able to see millions of stars up there."

She lifted her chin. "I hope so."

"I've only been to the cinema twice since arriving here," he offered.

"What picture did you see?"

"I don't remember the name. It was a Charlie Chaplin short film."

"He's quite amusing."

"Yes." They walked the half-block to the cinema and went inside. For the moment, Ella felt like she was back at home, in a delightful courtship.

***

After the picture ended, Garrett and Ella strolled back to her dormitory. Garrett smiled as he listened to her speak about the movie.

"I like the term belovedest, don't you? When Stella used that term, my ears perked up."

"It seems to assume there is more than one beloved, doesn't it?"

"It could, but it could also mean beloved in terms of family. That's how Stella referred to it."

"Yes, you're right."

"I just can't believe that Mary Pickford played both the

characters of Stella Maris and Unity, the orphan. I mean, they didn't look at all similar. And how do you think they filmed it with both in the same scenes?"

"Not sure but it is, after all, the 20th century. With modern motion pictures, anything's possible."

"Yes."

Garrett cleared his throat. "So does this mean you enjoyed the film?"

"Yes, I did. There is nothing like a good story to take one away from it all. And I almost never read novels because I'm always studying textbooks, but if I had more time, I certainly would."

"I enjoy reading."

"What kind of books do you like to read?"

"Modern literature. I like the *Tarzan of the Apes* series by Edgar Rice Burroughs. Quite fascinating."

"Was Tarzan an ape?"

He chuckled. "Well, no, he was actually a British boy whose parents died while they were living on an island and he was raised by the apes."

"Raised by apes? Sounds peculiar."

"I hear they might be making a motion picture about it."

"Then we'll have to see it when they do."

"Yes, we will."

The two continued walking in companionable silence.

Garrett pointed at the dark night sky and the millions of stars. "Beautiful. They look like tiny diamonds in the sky."

"Yes."

They passed the barrack that served as the Catholic

chapel. Ella stopped and made the Sign of the Cross. Garrett did the same.

Ella said, "Do you know that Our Blessed Mother is sometimes called Stella Maris?"

"Really?"

"Yes. It means 'star of the sea.'"

He nodded.

She took hold of his hand, and they began strolling. From how slowly she was moving one foot in front of the other, he wondered whether she was trying to prolong the evening or whether there was another reason she didn't want the night to end.

At her dorm barrack, she stopped, let go of his hand, and leaned against the side of the tent. Two medical volunteers walked towards the barrack, so Garrett stepped out of the way as the young women entered.

He inched closer to her. "I've really enjoyed our time together, Ella."

"Me too. It's been a lovely evening. Thank you so much for inviting me to the cinema." She straightened and again took hold of his hand.

"My...uh... pleasure."

He lifted her hand to his lips and kissed her palm. He released her hand and cupped his palms on her cheeks, then lightly kissed her lips. "Till tomorrow." He opened his eyes and stepped back.

Ella sighed. "Yes, till tomorrow."

Chapter Twenty-One
Familiar Image

Ella learned a few weeks later that the city of Lille was finally liberated by the Allies. She couldn't stop humming. The war was coming to an end.

Ella or Gary had found almost no spare time over the ensuing weeks, especially since so many of the staff had contracted influenza. Ella had been in and out of the influenza barrack but thankfully had not contracted the virus. Neither had Gary.

They attended Catholic Mass at the chapel two Sundays ago, just after their second kiss. Ella was more than pleased that Gary had known all the Latin responses. When they had knelt side by side at the rail and received Communion, Ella felt a spiritual bond to this man, who – she was sure – was meant to be her future husband.

Since they were now short-staffed, there was little time for leisure, so a passing wave or wink had to suffice for the time being.

Ella continued working in the OR doing much of the suturing. When she wasn't in the OR, she was treating minor injuries in the American barrack that served as the dining hall. That's where she was today, but Ella hoped she might have a few hours of leisure later in the afternoon.

Sr. Gladdie, the friendly, kind British nurse, was in charge today, and it always brightened Ella's day to work with the short-statured nurse.

Ella had just finished bandaging a head laceration on one of the soldiers when Sr. Gladdie said somberly, "Nurse Neumann, there's a soldier waiting on the far cot near the front door. He's got a deep shrapnel wound in his head, and it's bleeding profusely. I suggest you take the watch off the front of your apron and store it safely where it won't be soiled."

"Of course." Ella unpinned the timepiece from her apron, set it on the desk near the front door, and approached the soldier, who was holding a bloodied cloth to the top of his head. She greeted the soldier, then said, "Let's see what you've got there." She steadied herself as he took off the bandage, and the wound began bleeding, a few spurts jumping out at her and landing on her apron.

***

Garrett took off his cap and wiped his forehead. The sweat had been dripping into his eyes. He had just put the last soldier into the medical *camion* when he felt a red-hot sting in his shoulder, whipping him back against the vehicle. He glanced in the direction of the shot.

Two stretcher-bearers were trying to unarm an enemy soldier.

He touched the area where he had been shot. It was sticky with blood.

Moving with care to avoid further pain, he undid a few buttons and checked on the wound. It seeped blood but, thankfully, wasn't gushing. He stuffed his handkerchief next to the wound and raced across the field about fifty feet away to the two men trying to unarm the enemy soldier. He arrived as one of the stretcher-bearers yanked the gun away, but not before the enemy soldier looked up and stared at Garrett.

The man squinted, then said in German, "*Ich kenne Sei.*" *I know you.*

Garrett's heart pounded. In English, he said, "I don't understand you."

"I can tell by your eyes that you do understand me," he said in German. "You are a traitor." The man stared at the name on Garrett's uniform. "Brown? I don't think so."

One of the stretcher-bearers tied the man's hands behind his back.

"Take him away," Garrett said to the stretcher-bearers, ignoring what the soldier said.

But Garrett *had* recognized him as one of the men in his unit when he'd posed as a German officer. He would have to tell Collins that he no longer was safe in the field.

When he returned to the base hospital, he went to the dining hut that had been partially converted to a minor injury treatment area. He needed to get this wound looked after before he informed Collins that he was recognized in the field.

Ella had been working on and off at the dining hut, but he hoped she wasn't currently on duty. The wound was just below his large birthmark. If she saw it, she might suspect. Or she may not even remember the German officer who tried to escape.

No, he couldn't risk it. She definitely had seen it once, and she might remember, but he would quietly check the dining hut. He had vowed to tell her everything once the war was over. But the war wasn't over yet.

He opened the door quietly. Ella was across the room, her back toward him. *Thank goodness she doesn't see me. I'll just leave before she does and come back when she isn't on duty.* Just then, another soldier came in and slammed the door.

***

Ella had just finished cleaning and stitching a flesh wound when she heard the barrack door slam behind her. She turned. A soldier holding a cloth to his arm had just come through the door, and Gary stood beside him. Gary smiled.

She bid her patient goodbye and approached Gary wiping her hands on her apron. "This is a pleasant surprise."

"Just thought I'd drop by and see if you were busy." He stared at her apron, which by this time was a bloody mess. "I can tell you've been busy."

"I have."

The other soldier touched Ella's arm. "I need some help, Nurse."

"Of course." Turning toward Gary, she said, "I'm sorry. I *am* busy. But I should be free soon, if you want to go for a stroll."

"Yes, that would be fine."

***

That was a close one. However, Garrett would have to return when she was not on duty to have his shoulder wound stitched.

He walked across the suturing area to the small dining area and poured himself a cup of coffee. When he noticed another nurse come on duty to relieve Ella, he tried to think of a plan to return so the other nurse could clean and stitch up his wound.

Ella appeared to finish treating the soldier, then she approached him. "I'm finished now. Would you like to go for a walk?"

"If you give me about ten minutes, I'd be happy to go for a walk. I have something to attend to. Why don't you..."

"I think I'll eat something first. Then you can go do whatever you need to do, and I'll remain here."

She isn't making this easy.

"That sounds good," he said. "Shall I meet you back here or somewhere else?"

"After I eat, I was hoping to take a stroll on the beach. It's a beautiful day. Can you meet me at the *funiculaire* in about an hour?"

Perfect. "Yes, I can." He leaned in to kiss her cheek. "I'll see you soon."

Garrett left, crossed the street and ran the two blocks to the main building. He needed to report to Collins that he was no longer safe in the field, that someone had recognized him.

Thankfully, the meeting was short and to the point with Collins urging him to get stitched up soon. That was his plan. He returned to the dining hall and peered in through the front door. Ella was nowhere to be found.

He approached the short, middle-aged nurse at the desk. "Ma'am?"

She turned and smiled widely. "Yes, Corporal?" Her name tag read "*Sr. Gladdie Caufield.*"

"Sister, I have a flesh wound that needs to be cleaned and sutured. Would you be able to do that?"

"I'd be happy to help you. Follow me."

He followed her to a cot nearby, sat down and unbuttoned and took off his shirt.

"Oh, that looks nasty, Corporal."

"It's not bad. Hardly bled at all. Just need to have it cleaned and sutured."

As she cleaned and applied pressure, he winced.

"Sorry. I'll be finished in a few moments." She paused. "Say, that's an unusual birthmark on your shoulder. Don't think I've ever seen one so large."

"I'm told it's one of a kind."

"I'm sure it is."

***

Ella had almost made it to her dormitory to change into a clean skirt and blouse when she went to check the time. Looking down at the front of her apron, her timepiece wasn't there. *I left it on the desk!* She turned back toward the dining hut to retrieve the timepiece. She opened the door and stopped. There, sitting on a cot with his back to her was Gary. Sr. Gladdie appeared to be stitching a wound on his shoulder.

She opened her mouth to say hello, but they began to speak so she closed it again.

"Why did you wait so long to have this sutured?" Sr. Gladdie asked.

"Oh, well, I just haven't had time since I returned from the field."

Instead of making her presence known, she tiptoed to the desk to pick up her watch without saying a word and took a backward glanced toward the pair.

There on Gary's shoulder was a strange-looking birthmark. She tilted her head and stared at the peculiar shape of it, searching her memory. She had seen that birthmark before, but where?

Chapter Twenty-Two
Awkward Conversation

The entire walk back to her dormitory, questions swirled in Ella's mind. Where had she seen that birthmark before? It certainly wasn't on Gary because she had never seen his naked chest/shoulders before. But she *had* seen that very pattern before; she was certain of it.

And how had he gotten the wound? She couldn't see much of the injury, especially since the birthmark took most of her attention. Even so, he had been hurt when he came to see her earlier. Why hadn't he asked *her* to suture the wound? After all, she was an expert at suturing.

The birthmark. Maybe he was self-conscious about it.

No, that couldn't be it. Ella had seen that birthmark before. Maybe she should just ask him.

She made it to her dorm in time to change quickly.

***

Garrett thanked the nurse and made his way to the *funiculaire* station.

When he reached the station, Ella was not yet there. Within moments, she was strolling up the walkway. She gave him a too-quick smile.

He tipped his cap. "Hello, Ella."

"Hello."

She didn't make eye contact.

"Is everything all right?" he asked.

"Yes, yes, I'm...fine."

They took the *funiculaire* in silence and without her usual comments about the beautiful scenery. She stared at the walls of the *funiculaire* instead of the water, cliff and town below. When they got off the tram, he went to take her arm and that was the first time she made eye contact.

She took hold of his hand, and they walked to the beach. The beach was crowded on this warm, sunny day, and tiny stones and sand made it difficult to walk.

A young boy ran across their path, and she held onto Garrett's arm so he wouldn't run into the boy.

"You seem quiet today, Ella."

She nodded. "I was trying to remember where I had seen...something."

"Something?"

***

She was just about to ask him about his birthmark when she heard girls on a blanket chatting nearby.

"Did you hear?" one girl asked.

"What?" another girl said.

"One of the German POWs escaped last evening," the first girl said.

"They should step up security here."

"I know."

Ella drew in a breath, and her heart skipped a beat. She remembered where she had seen that birthmark.

***

Garrett listened to the girls speaking about the German

POW escaping. Ella gasped, and her mouth opened. She remained still and silent for a few moments, her face pale.

"What's wrong, Ella?"

She opened her mouth to speak, then stared at him.

Suddenly, she practically yanked on his hand and pulled him away from the crowds.

"We need privacy," she said bluntly.

"We do?" he asked.

"Yes."

Her tone seemed too serious. And she was squeezing his hand so much that it was starting to hurt. Her entire body seemed to be shaking. *What is going on here?*

He had to practically run to keep up with her as she pulled him toward the lonely cliff, where there were no people.

She finally released his hand and leaned against the cliff, her gaze facing downward. A salty, warm breeze blew locks of her hair across her sullen features. Distant laughter and playful voices stood in stark contrast to her somber mood. He'd never seen her like this.

"Is... everything all right, Ella?"

"No."

"No?"

"Or should I say, *nicht wirklich?*"

"What are you talking about?"

"Would you please remove your shirt?"

His chest tightened, and he shook his head. Somehow, she knew about the birthmark. He fought the impulse to just leave. But what could he do now? Respond with humor. "Well, gee, Ella, isn't it a bit early in our relationship for that sort of behavior? That's not a request I'd expect from a young lady."

Her eyes narrowed a bit more. "Gary – or whatever your name is – please remove your shirt."

Deflated, he unbuttoned his shirt and slipped it off his shoulders. "Anything else, madam?"

She stared at his birthmark, and her lips quivered. "What is... your...real name?" she asked, her tone sharp but on the verge of tears.

He whispered, even though they were alone. "Garrett Smith, also known as Gerhard Schmidt, German officer."

"I knew it. You're a double agent, a spy!" She collapsed against the stone of the cliff, her hand pressing her chest.

"I am a spy, but for the Allies. I am not a double agent." Desperate to convince her, he reached for her arm. His fingers grazed her sleeve, but he shouldn't touch her now. She wasn't sure about him. She doubted him. He planted his hand on the wall of the cliff behind her, leaning closer as he tried to explain. "When you first met me....I was a German officer, but I was working undercover. Right now, I'm a Canadian corporal, which is closer to what I really am, except my actual rank is Major."

She shook her head, waved her arms and pushed past him. "I can't think about this right now. I need to get back to the dorm."

"Yes, by all means." They walked back to the *funiculaire* station to take the tram through the cliff. She stayed in front of him.

She didn't glance back to see if he was following, but she finally stopped and turned. She stood still, tears filling her eyes. "Was... *everything*... you told me... a lie?"

"No, Ella. My feelings for you and what I told you about my family is all true." His heart was breaking. He hated to see her so sad. She didn't respond. She stomped away toward the *funiculaire* station.

He sighed and stopped. He would need to give her time. Nearby, children played and yelled while making a sandcastle. Suddenly, one of the smaller boys kicked the castle apart.

Chapter Twenty-Three
Heartache

Ella tossed and turned all night, biting her lip to keep from sobbing. There was no use in disturbing the other girls in the dormitory barrack.

News that the war would soon end did not lift her mood. Instead, her heart felt empty. Gary – Garrett – told her he was an Allied spy and not a German officer. What should she believe? Was he really working for the Allies? Or was he actually a German spy? Maybe she should ask Collins. If Collins didn't know anything about Garrett's double life, that would most certainly indicate he was German.

She lowered her head. No, he couldn't be a German spy. He wouldn't have protected her on the trip to Lille a few months ago. He had to be telling her the truth. But what of his declaration of love for her?

No, she couldn't continue her relationship with Garrett until she had this all sorted out.

She threw off the covers and proceeded to get ready for the day. She would start the day off suturing in the OR and then spend the second half of the day in the minor injuries tent.

Exiting the tent, she put her headscarf on and passed the church barrack. Usually, she blessed herself, but today she was in a rush. Why would God allow her to fall in love with him? She had never before given her heart to any man. She had never even kissed a man before Garrett.

It was a cloudy, threatening-to-rain morning. She

tromped the lengthy blocks to the main building and the OR. She kept her gaze down, not wanting to look anybody in the eye. From the voices around her, there were many medical personnel out and about.

"Ella? Please, let me explain."

Garrett's voice. She stiffened and glanced up. Garrett approached her from the main building's porch. "Please talk to me, Ella."

"I don't believe there's anything to say, Corporal Brown," she leaned in close and whispered, "or should I say Smith?"

She tried to move around him to enter the building, but he stepped in her way. "Please, just listen to me. Give me two minutes."

Pursing her lips and crossing her arms, she stepped back and tapped her foot. "I'm listening."

He took her by the arm to an area beside the main building, where they would have privacy.

"I love you, Ella. That has not changed. I love you more than life itself, and I'd be honored to have you as my wife."

She scoffed.

"Please, Ella. I couldn't tell you anything about my..." – he leaned close and whispered – "espionage work." He paused. "Even if we were married, I wouldn't have been able to tell you that information."

He would lie to her even when married? "Wa...why?" Her voice cracked. "Why...should I believe...you? You were very... convincing... as a German officer."

"Because I'm telling the truth...now."

She turned away and said nothing for several minutes. Finally, she faced him. "I don't think we should continue spending time together."

He inched toward her, and she stepped back. "Ella?"

***

Ella made eye contact, and the emotions Garrett saw in those piercing blue eyes broke his heart. Hurt, disappointment, estrangement, sadness. Surely, she had to understand why he couldn't break his cover – even for her.

"Please promise me." He took her by the shoulder.

She lifted her shoulders and stepped back. "What?"

"That you won't reveal my true identity."

"You need not worry. I'm not even sure what your true identity is."

Garrett sometimes wondered that himself. "I already told you. I'm working for the Allies."

"Yes, so you say."

"Please, Ella."

***

Ella opened her mouth to speak but closed it. The hurt and disappointment were too raw right now. If anything, she needed time. "I can't – I can't do this right now. It's too painful." She turned to leave, and he touched her arm.

"I understand. But please know that I'd marry you this moment if you were agreeable. I truly want to spend the rest of my life with you."

Ella's eyes watered. *I can't deal with this now.* "Please, I need to go." He stepped back, and she rushed off, trying to get her wits about her before she started her shift in the OR.

Chapter Twenty-Four
Back on the Field

It started to rain as Garrett watched Ella run off. He swallowed hard. *Well, that could've gone better.*

She loved him; he was certain of that. She wouldn't be so upset if she didn't have feelings for him.

He controlled his urge to run after her. It would take time for her to adjust, and he would have to be patient – not one of his strong traits. Perhaps in a few days, she might feel less hurt and realize that as a spy, he couldn't have been totally honest with her.

She had said she didn't really know him. At times, Garrett struggled with figuring himself out. But he was more certain of his love for her than he'd been about anything in his life.

Returning to his duties, he picked up the trash can to deposit it in the rubbish bin.

One of Collins' messengers approached him. "Corporal?"

"Yes?"

"The lieutenant needs to see you. He says it's urgent."

"Very well."

He finished dumping the trash, then made his way to the main building. Garrett stepped onto the porch and then into the foyer. After removing his cap, he knocked and went in. He put the cap under his arm. The secretary looked up. "He's waiting for you in his office, Corporal. Go ahead in."

"Thank you."

As a courtesy, he rapped on Collins' door before swinging it open. Collins sat at his desk, the stick phone's receiver at his ear and his mouth near the mouthpiece. The older man jotted down notes on a piece of paper. "There's no other way?" Collins ignored Garrett, so Garrett decided to sit down. More questions from Collins to the person on the other end of the stick phone, "When?" and "Very well." Collins wrote more letters – or were they numbers? – and hung the receiver back onto its hook.

The lieutenant finally lifted his head. "Thank you for coming."

"What's so urgent?"

"I need you back in the field."

Garrett straightened. "Oh?"

"Just for this one last trip." Collins stood up, picked up a photograph from his desk and handed it to Garrett.

"What's this?"

"This is a reconnaissance photo of one of the German airfields in Belgium." He pointed to a large tube-like structure.

"A zeppelin," Garrett noted.

"And the rest of these are airplanes. A lot of them. Our contact on the ground in Abbeville was just killed. I need you to get this photograph to our man in Lille. He'll take it from there."

"Yes, very well." Garrett stopped. "The contact on the ground in Abbeville isn't the Australian chap that housed me, is it?"

"Yes, I'm afraid it is."

Garrett felt an ache in his chest. *Requiescat in pace.* "Madelaine is probably heartbroken."

"I'm sure."

"Look, I know someone recognized you the last time you were in the field, but this photograph must be in the hands of the Allies by this evening. With agents and resources decreasing, you're the only one at hand with any espionage experience. Can you do it?"

"Of course."

"Get to Lille by this evening, deliver the photograph and return immediately. Don't use well-traveled roads."

Collins stood, so Garrett did the same. Collins slipped the photograph into an envelope. He reached across the desk and handed it to Garrett. "This photograph is essential to the Allies' continuing victory, Garrett. Guard it with your life."

"Yes, sir."

"There's an autocar in front of the building. You're to report to the hospital in Lille and give the photograph to the Allied commander. Return immediately."

"Yes, sir."

Before leaving Collins' office, Garrett took the photograph and placed it in the hidden compartment of his cap. He then saluted the lieutenant and as he turned to leave, he heard, "Godspeed."

Hand to the doorknob, he nodded, then swung the door open.

He wished he could talk to Ella before he left, but she

was still likely not talking to him, nor could he mention what he was about to do anyway.

***

Garrett drove the autocar towards Lille. Up until this point in the war, he didn't think much about danger. He just did his job without reflecting. But now? He didn't care about the danger, but he did care deeply about – loved – Ella and didn't want to cause her more grief.

He had just made it to the outskirts of Lille when an oval metal – *dear God, a grenade* – dropped onto the road in front of him. His world now moving in slow motion, he steered the vehicle away from it. The grenade went off beside him, with a deafening blast and a shower of earth. Smoke filled the air — filled his lungs. Coughing, eyes stinging, he jerked the steering wheel, hoping to swerve away from—rolling smoke revealed a tree in his path, but too late—the autocar slammed to a stop. His head slammed the dashboard.

He jerked his head upright, lifting it from the steering wheel and blinked as he struggled to regain his bearings. Had he lost consciousness for a moment? Smoke still filled the air. Something cracked hard on the back of his head. Everything turned dark.

Garrett lay on the floor of a moving *camion*. His head ached and throbbed. A man coughed. Another man moaned. Despite his pain, he allowed the moving of the *camion* to lull him back to unconsciousness.

***

Garrett roused and rubbed the back of his head. His head throbbed like there was a metal stake going through it. Every inch of his body was wet. *What the...* The stench of human excrement assaulted his nostrils. He groaned.

In German, he heard, "Ah, it's so nice to see you joining the party, Major."

He blinked his eyes. In front of him stood a man grinning from ear to ear. Where had he seen him? His eyes widened as he recognized him. *The man in the field.*

Continuing to speak also in German, another man said, "We make it a priority to capture traitors and spies, both of which you are. You're scheduled to be executed by firing squad on Friday. We were pleased to be able to tell your commander this information."

Garrett tried to draw in a breath, but he had no strength and the stench of urine gagged him.

"And we have the secret information that you were supposed to deliver." He laughed.

His wet head indicated that his cap wasn't there. It must've fallen off at some point after his capture. But he was sure they were bluffing. They would certainly have been more specific about the photograph *if* they had it.

"But first, we're going to make your last days ones of extreme pain and suffering."

Pain and suffering? He had spent most of the war in dangerous circumstances and had escaped death already. He wasn't afraid of pain.

Ella's face appeared in his mind. His heart ached. If he hadn't met her, it wouldn't hurt so much that he was facing death. He wasn't afraid of death. God was merciful and would forgive his sins. But he was afraid of how his death would affect *her*. Perhaps she would still be mad at him. No, she would not still be mad. She loved him. He was certain of that.

A flash of pain sliced through his cheek, then hard metal cracked his already injured skull. One German ripped the shirt from his body. Another kicked him, turning him onto his stomach. Then the lash of a sharp whip ripped some skin from his back. The words from the Kilmer poem reverberated in his mind. He clenched onto something wet in the mud to keep from crying out. That was what they wanted, for him to cry out and to give them information. But he would not do so, no matter the pain. *God, please help me.* With the searing pain ripping his flesh, he recited the Kilmer poem in his mind. *My shoulders ache be...neath my pack, Lie easier, Cross, up...on his back. I march with feet that burn... and smart, Tread, Holy Feet, upon my heart.*

Garrett lifted his head and glanced at his persecutors. *Men... shout at me who may not speak, they scourged... Thy back and smote Thy cheek.*

Another blow to his cheek. He grunted, blood and mud smearing his face. *I may not lift a hand to clear my eyes of salty drops that sear, then shall my fickle soul forget... Thy Agony of Bloody Sweat?*

His persecutors stretched his arms out on either side. Now sprawled on his stomach in the mud, his hands burned. Writhing in pain, struggling to breathe, he inched his face away from the mud and glimpsed his torturers stabbing his wrists and hands with what appeared to be a screwdriver. *My...rifle hand is stiff and numb, from thy... pierced palm red rivers come.*

Cruel laughter rang out, the men mocking him. *Lord, thou didst suffer more...for...me than all the hosts of...land and sea. So, let me render back again, this millionth of thy gift, Amen.*

Father, forgive them for they know not what they do.

Another blow to his head and everything dissolved into darkness.

Chapter Twenty-Five
Another Trip to the Front

By day's end, Ella's heart had softened enough to make her want to talk with Garrett. After her shift in the OR, she made her way to the POW barrack. Garrett wasn't there. Her feet ached from being on them all day, but she continued searching. A spitting rain had begun, and thunder cracked in the distance.

She couldn't find him at the dining barrack, nor was he in any of the usual places. The last spot she would check was the Canadian sleeping barrack for enlisted men. She asked one of the soldiers standing there if he had seen Corporal Brown. The man indicated that he had not.

On her way to the main building, one of Collins' men approached her. "The lieutenant needs to see you as soon as possible, Miss."

"Very well." She followed the man to the main building and had to nearly run to keep up with him. Regardless of why Collins wanted to see her, she would ask him about Garrett.

Still in the lead, the soldier stomped across the porch and disappeared into the building. Trailing a few seconds behind, Ella mounted the porch steps just as the sky let loose with torrential rains.

She crossed the foyer and as she opened the door, the

secretary lifted her chin and met Ella's gaze. "Come in, Nurse Neumann."

"Thank you."

"You may go ahead in."

As Ella entered his office, Collins stood. He motioned for her to take a seat in front of the desk. They both sat down.

"First, I need your help again. I know you're not a trained spy, and the other mission was a one-time thing, but I've got another mission and no one more suitable to do it."

"Me? I don't understand."

"A high-ranking Allied officer has been captured and is currently being held in the same German POW camp you visited a few months ago."

"That's awful." She thought back to the inhumane conditions she found at the other camp.

"However, that POW camp has moved to just inside the Belgian border."

"Oh?"

"Yes, we need you to confirm that he is there and assess his condition."

"I...don't...know. When...will this happen?"

"As soon as possible, 0400."

Checking her timepiece, Ella said, "That's only six hours from now."

"Correct." Collins sat straight in his chair. "I've received information that this high-ranking officer will be put to death within the next few days."

"Oh, no." She gripped the arms of the chair.

"Well, will you do this?"

She opened her mouth, then closed it. She wanted to say yes because Collins obviously needed her. The reason she volunteered was to help people, and this captured high-ranking officer needed her help.

"Miss Neumann? I'm sorry to put extra stress on you, but I need an answer immediately."

Leaning forward in the chair, she said, "Yes, I will do it. You want me to confirm he's there and that's it?"

"Yes, and the name of the officer."

"That's all?"

"Yes. Once we have confirmation, then we will attack the camp in hopes of a rescue."

Ella's heart raced. What if the German guard recognized her? What if von Kirchbach recognized her? What if... "Very well then. But I would ask only that Corporal Brown drive me, like last time."

Collins cleared his throat. "Corporal Brown. If...if he's...." He stared at her for a full two seconds before finishing his sentence. "Well, if he's available. Yes." He cleared his throat again and straightened a notepad on his desk. "Haven't seen him all day."

"No one seems to have seen him all day, sir." Ella's chest tightened. Should she ask about Garrett now? She took a deep breath and released it. "Speaking of Garrett, I know that Garrett is a double agent."

The lieutenant's eyes widened. "Excuse me?"

"Garrett told me."

"If he told you, then I'm sure he also told you that he's *not* a double agent, but that he's working for the Allies."

She lowered her head. "Yes, he did say that. I didn't know whether to believe him."

"Well, it's true." He stood up. "I'm sure...he will...um... show up at some point." Collins seemed to be forcing a smile. "Then I'll tell him he'll be driving you. So, tomorrow at 0345 in front of the main building. A German nurse's uniform will also be in the *camion*."

"Thank you, sir."

"Thank you, Nurse Neumann."

She slept fitfully and after a few hours of sleep, woke and prepared for her trip to the border. She was worried about Garrett, but hopefully she would see him when he drove her to the border. Part of her wished that he had left the bicycle in her care. She rather enjoyed riding it, and it took much less time to get to the main building or anywhere on campus. But he had told her others would be using it.

She walked to the main building and despite the darkness of the morning, a *camion* was visible, parked in front. Even though she was still angry with him, her heart skipped a beat. She would finally be able to speak with Garrett.

Ella couldn't make out the person behind the wheel until she was practically in front of it. She drew in a breath when she saw who the driver was: Lieutenant Collins.

Upon seeing her, he started the engine and got out. He assisted her into the passenger seat.

As he began to drive, Collins turned and stared at her, his expression odd. He kept glancing at her, then back toward the road.

Why wasn't Garrett driving her? Why was Collins acting strangely? Something was not right. "What's wrong, sir? Why isn't Garrett driving me to the border?"

"I wasn't sure last night when I told you about this mission, but we now believe that Garrett is the high-ranking officer that was captured."

Ella drew in a breath and held her hand to her chest to calm her beating heart. "Captured? I don't understand. He hasn't been in the field for at least a week."

"He was intercepted on his way to deliver a...um...message to Lille. We're relatively certain that he is the high-ranking officer who was captured."

Ella gasped. "No!" Images of the Allied officers lying in their own filth with no food or water – she couldn't bear to think of Garrett in that condition.

"We don't know where they've taken him, but I have good information that it's the same camp that used to be near Lille. As I told you last evening, it's been moved to the Belgian border. This is why you're coming. You need to verify he's there and inform me about how many enemy soldiers are there."

"Verify? If he's there, I'm going to try to get him released."

The lieutenant kept his gaze forward as he drove, but he shook his head. "Miss Neumann, if they have captured him, they will *not* release him. I have a team on standby prepared to rescue him and the others."

"That's good, right?"

"Yes, but they won't be ready for the rescue operation until tomorrow. So all you need to do is confirm."

"What if you can't get the team ready in time?"

"We have to take that chance, Miss Neumann."

"Why? Why not just go in and rescue all the men?"

"Because we need to make sure it's not a suicide mission for our men executing the rescue. The enemy is desperate and resorting to killing as many of the Allied officers as they can. You yourself testified to the condition of starvation at that camp in Lille."

Ella fell silent, and a sob caught in her throat. She tried to relax against the seat, but she couldn't, not at a time like this. *Think, think.* The last time she had been at that enemy camp, she had discovered that the German officer whose life she had saved was the commander. *Yes, that's it!* She straightened.

"What's wrong?" Collins asked.

"I'm fine, just thinking." Was von Kirchbach still there? If he *was* there, perhaps that guard who tried to have his way with her was there too. No, she couldn't think of that. She had to focus on von Kirchbach. He had promised her that he would do anything for her. She saved his life. He said "anything." But what if he didn't agree to release Garrett? What if he no longer cared that Ella had saved his life? No, she could *not* despair – not now – not when Garrett needed her most.

"Dr. Dubois tells me you attended The Woman's Medical College of Pennsylvania in Philadelphia."

"Yes, that's correct, sir."

"Only one year?"

"Half a year. I wish I could have finished."

"That's too bad. Why did you quit school?"

"To help support my family and my younger siblings."

"I see."

She wished the lieutenant would stop talking. There were too many variables swirling around in her mind. Was

Garrett even alive? And if he was, was he injured? Would von Kirchbach help her? Should she just wait for Collins to try to rescue Garrett, if he was there?

"Are you hoping to?"

"Hoping to what?"

"Finish medical school?"

"Yes, sir, I was hoping to."

More small talk and more short answers. Ella had hoped that the three hours would seem longer. But before she knew it, Collins drove up to the place close to the border and stopped. The lieutenant got out of the *camion* and moved toward the passenger side of the vehicle. He opened the door and assisted Ella down.

They went to the back of the *camion*. Collins reached in and took out the bicycle. He then left her alone so she could dress.

Ella pulled her German nurse's uniform from a bag. Her hands trembled, preventing her from slipping a button through the buttonhole of her blouse. She tried again. And failed. What if she couldn't dress herself? She couldn't—wouldn't—ask Collins for assistance. With a determined shove, the button slid into place despite her trembling hands, then the next, and the next. Finally, she managed to dress herself in the German nurse's uniform. Wait—she pulled the glasses from the apron pocket and put them on. Yes, now she was ready.

She crawled out of the *camion*. Her shoes hit the cold, hard ground, and her heart thumped harder. This was really happening. Garrett was a POW, and she needed to rescue him.

She joined Collins at the side of the truck. The man surely *was* a giant, although it was hard to notice most of the time, since he was usually sitting or briefly standing in courtesy to her.

"Godspeed, Miss Neumann. The new location of the POW camp is just over the border. Take your bicycle down this road, and you'll see an old farmhouse. The captives are likely being held outside somewhere. You know what to do, correct?"

"Confirm if Garrett is there, then return."

"You're there simply as a German nurse giving medical attention to the prisoners. I'll be right here waiting for you. You're not to take more than three hours."

"What if I'm caught? What if they discover who I am?"

"Say nothing. If you're not back in three hours, I will ready men to recover you and Garrett before he's executed."

She gave no reply other than a nod and then turned toward the bike. Another plan brewed in her mind.

Ella pedaled the bike quickly over the dirt road and to the enemy POW camp. When she arrived, she got off the bicycle. This time, a guard stood on the porch of a bombed-out farmhouse. The sun was just rising, and the area was shrouded in a sleepy silence. A thick forest edged the property of the camp. She avoided eye contact and in German, she said, "I'm here to give medical attention to the prisoners."

He mumbled something, and she looked up. It wasn't the same man! *Thank you, God.* This guard waved her onto the porch and allowed her inside. In German, he said, "First door on the right." Ella stepped inside the foyer, then approached the first door on the right. She knocked.

Inside was Mrs. Hoffmann, who recognized her from her previous trip.

In German, the woman said, "Miss Müller, the prisoners are outside in tents behind the house." She waved her on without accompanying her. Ella scanned the hallway as she moved through it for indication that von Kirchbach was still stationed there, but there was none.

The sun was now bathing the area in light. Four tattered tents stood behind the farmhouse, and a barn behind them, the nickering of horses inside.

The first tattered tent held no one, and Ella let out a huge breath.

Inside the second tattered tent, after her eyes became accustomed to the darkness, she knelt down and inspected each of the five officers.

Garrett was not among them. As before, these men were all semi-conscious and in filthy conditions. If it was possible, these prisoners suffered in worse conditions than the prisoners at the camp near Lille.

Ella wouldn't want animals to be treated like this. She hated that she wasn't able to spend more time to actually help them, but all she could do was to give each one a sip of water and some soothing words. Then she was on to the next tent.

The third tent held two men, both of whom seemed to be conscious and in fair condition, despite the mud they sat in. She spoke in English. "Sirs, I am here to help you. I have water and if you are wounded, I can clean and bandage your wounds."

"Y'all are most kind." A young soldier leaned forward, pressing one palm to the ground in an attempt to get to his feet. He winced, his other hand shooting to his outstretched leg. Blood soaked the thigh of his trousers. "Sorry, Miss."

Reaching out her hand to steady him, she lowered him back down. "No need, sir."

The other young man, a Canadian corporal, smiled at her. His name tag said, "Dolan." He shook his head. "You speak English extremely well for a German nurse."

She whispered, "I'm American, but please keep that quiet."

"Very well. Miss, if you could check the other tents for the man who traveled here in the same *camion* as us. His name is Corporal Brown, and he had a nasty wound on the back of his head."

Ella gasped.

"The Germans have beaten him mercilessly. They called him a traitor. He needs more help than we do."

The young American man said, "Y'all need to go help him then. Go, ma'am." His Southern accent had been music to her ears.

She nodded. "Thank you. I will." She moved toward the flap of the tent to leave.

Dolan said, "I overheard one of the guards saying that he will be executed this afternoon. And I suspect we will be as well."

"No!"

"Please, go tend to that man. The least he can have is some comfort before he's executed."

She walked fifteen or so steps to the next tent. Opening the flaps, she prayed, on the one hand, *not* to find Garrett because finding him would mean he was critically injured.

On the other hand, she hoped that she *would* find Garrett. Then she would know either way.

She kept the flap open to shine light on the inside of the tent. Only one man lay on his back, his bloodied and bruised head flopped to one side, and blood-stained rips in his clothing showed where they had beaten him.

Squinting, Ella read the letters on his name tag out loud. "B, r, o –" This *was* Garrett! *Oh, no, no. What if he is already –*

At that moment, his chest rose and fell with a breath. He was alive! She released a long breath, now aware that she had been holding it. She dropped down beside him and reached for his wrist. Checking his pulse, it was surprisingly strong. She took a cloth from her bag and dunked it in the clean water pail she kept outside the tents, then knelt beside him and tenderly cleaned his wounds.

When she lifted his face, he moaned. His right cheek was so badly injured that it had sunk right into his mouth with a few of his beautiful, bottom teeth now broken and poking through. His nasal cavity was also visible. *Dear God, what have you been through, Garrett?*

For now, she could only cleanse the area and cover it to try to keep it from getting infected. When she finished cleaning and bandaging his face, she gave him a tetanus hypodermic and then morphine for his pain. Examining the rest of his body, she kept gasping each time she found a new injury. His hands had been poked or stabbed with something, so she cleaned them of the blood and mud as best she could and wrapped cloth bandages around them.

She opened up his shirt to find more open wounds, took her time in cleaning them and covering them, but there were too many, and she ran out of bandages before she could finish. When she turned him on his side to clean his back, Garrett moaned again.

Her heart wrenching, she whispered in his ear, "Sorry, Garrett."

***

Garret roused and struggled to open his heavy eyes. He lay on his side, a cold cloth on his back. It stung and he wanted to remove it, but his body ached too much for him to lift even a finger.

How many days had passed? One? Two? His eyelids felt like someone was clamping them shut, but he managed to crack them open.

Ella's face. Hovering above him. No, it couldn't be. He had hoped for death to come quickly. Maybe it had. Maybe God had allowed him to see Ella's face at the moment of his death. His pain had lessened.

"Garrett? It's me, Ella," she whispered.

He managed to nod but felt weak, nauseated, and dizzy. This all seemed *so* real. He could even smell her lilac perfume.

"I'm going to try to get you out of here."

When she lifted his head to give him a sip of water, his heavy eyelids relaxed, and he opened them. This was no dream, but he had no energy to be happy.

His stomach hurt, and his lips tingled. He opened his mouth to vomit the mouthful of water she had given him.

All he could do was thank God that he was allowed to see Ella again. But if she *was* here, then she was also in danger.

"Dan...ger..." was all he could say.

"Yes, I know."

"Dan...ger..."

"I shall be back in a few moments."

"Don't...leave..."

"I must, but I shall return."

"Sor...ry..."

"No, I'm sorry, Garrett. I love you."

"Love... you..."

"I know."

Chapter Twenty-Six
Promises, Promises

Ella made Garrett as comfortable as she could, said a prayer to every saint she could think of that he wouldn't die before she returned, then made her way to the farmhouse. With each step, she moved closer to the point of no return. She stopped at Mrs. Hoffman's office to inquire whether Major von Kirchbach was still the commander of this camp.

"He is. Why do you ask?" she replied in German.

"I wish to speak with him; that is all," Ella said in German.

"He's arranging for a firing squad for three of these men. They're going to be executed at noon."

Ella bit down on her lip to keep from responding. If Garrett was to be executed at noon, Collins wouldn't have time to rescue him. This confirmed what she had to do. What was the worst that could happen? It didn't matter because she had to try. "I need to see the major immediately please," she said in German.

The woman pushed the button of an intercom, then pointed Ella to the office across the foyer. A soldier stood guard and stepped aside to allow her to open the door. As she held onto the doorknob, the guard left, and another guard appeared to be coming on duty.

Ella turned the knob and swung open the door. The man behind the desk lifted his chin and looked up over his reading glasses. He stood up and motioned for her to take a seat at his desk, then sat down himself. In German, he asked, "What can I do for you, *fraulein*?"

Von Kirchbach's appearance was much different than he was at the POW ward. He was a handsome, well-built man in his forties with graying blond hair.

"Do... you... recognize me, sir?" she asked in German. She took off the glasses.

He tilted his head, then squinted as if something about her resonated in him. Then he said in German, "I...don't..."

Suddenly, he straightened in his chair and gasped and spoke in German. "You are the *fraulein* who saved my life! It is a pleasure to see you again." He reached out and shook her hand, then as if comprehending who she was, frowned.

In English, he asked, "You veren't a *fraulein* ven you saved my life, no?" He paused and stared at her. "And vy are you dressed as a German nurse?"

"I am... here to minister... to the Allied officers." Her heart raced, and she rubbed her sweaty palms together. "The only way I could do so was to dress in a German nursing uniform."

"But vy are you here in my office?"

She stood, as if that would give her the courage she'd need. "As you may recall, you promised me anything because I saved your life."

He squinted. "And what is it that you vant?"

"Well..."

He leaned forward. "Yes?"

"One of the officers here is my fiancé."

"Ah," he said, then lowered his head. "No, I cannot—"

"You *can* do anything, sir. You *can* release him. The war is ending."

He got up and came around the desk and leaned close to her, whispering, in German, "My dear, what you are asking is difficult. If I do that, then I shall be seen as a traitor. I could also be executed." He paused. "Which officer is your fiancé?"

"Major Gerhard Schmidt, true name, Major Garrett Smith," she said quietly.

He straightened, pounded the desk with his hand and shouted, "Absolutely not! He is a traitor! He will be facing a firing squad at noon!"

"Please, I beg you." If he asked her to kneel in front of him and beg, she would.

He paced the room for several minutes while Ella fidgeted in her chair. While he paced, there was still hope. The silence in the room reached out and seemed to strangle her to the point she couldn't breathe.

Then, without saying a word, he returned to his desk chair and sat down, his shoulders slumped. Ella remained silent. While she waited, he wrote on a piece of paper. *Why is he writing when I'm waiting for an answer?*

"I simply cannot do as you request," he said in heavily-accented English.

Her mouth fell open, and tears rushed to her eyes. "Please, sir. Please. You promised you'd do anything for me!"

"Guard, come in here immediately!" he shouted in German.

A guard opened the door almost immediately, his head tilted in confusion. "*Ja?*" In German, von Kirchbach said,

"Take her to the tent with the traitor, chain her to his shackles!"

"Yes, sir," the guard responded in German.

"No, please," she yelled. "Please don't do this!" The guard grabbed hold of her arm and started to drag her out of the office.

Suddenly, von Kirchbach yelled in German, "Wait!"

The guard and Ella turned to face von Kirchbach. He approached them, a frown plastered across his face. He stood over her, his glaring eyes piercing her already wounded heart.

She couldn't believe this. Grabbing his arm, she yelled, "Are you so heartless? Don't you understand that you wouldn't be here today if it weren't for me saving your life?"

"Take her away!" von Kirchbach bellowed.

This was not how she envisioned her life. Ella began to weep. The war would soon end, but rather than be free to marry and begin her life with Garrett, she would be imprisoned with him until the Germans executed him this afternoon.

When they reached Garrett's tent, the guard pulled her close to him, and she cried out.

As if this nightmare weren't enough, she now stared into the face of the guard who had tried to kiss her a few months ago. She twisted and tried to release herself from his grasp, but he was too strong.

He leered at her and in German, said, "Well, my little *fraulein*, I remember you. You are very pretty, especially without your glasses." He pulled off her headscarf and ran his hands through her hair.

"Please don't do this," she said in German. When the man continued and leaned down to kiss her, her eyes darted around. Would no one help her this time?

Unwilling to give in without a fight, Ella kicked him in the groin.

He screamed, crossed his legs, releasing her to hold his hands to the area.

She ran toward the office. Mrs. Hoffmann stopped her. In German, Ella said, "Please help me."

Mrs. Hoffmann stared at the guard in the distance and nodded. In German, she called the guard and told him to report to the commandant, that *she* would take the prisoner back to the tent.

The woman roughly took Ella by the arm and marched her back to the tent. She opened the flap, tossed her in, and Ella sprawled onto the wet ground beside Garrett. He roused but was silent. Mrs. Hoffmann secured a heavy shackle around her wrist, then took Garrett's shackles and connected the two of them. Ella shook so hard that the woman had difficulty connecting the chains.

Mrs. Hoffmann left, and the situation weighed heavily on Ella's shoulders and her heart, which was pounding a mile a minute. She was finding it hard to catch her breath and had to will herself to calm down. She finally took a few deep breaths in and out.

Instead of getting von Kirchbach to release Garrett, he was going to be executed. She had no idea what would happen to her. But at least that guard was gone.

God, if you allow us to get out of this situation, I will do anything you want me to do.

Scanning the dark tent, she searched for something, anything she might be able to use to open the locks on the chains. If she only had a way to get a message to Lieutenant Collins. Even if she could get a message to him, he already told her that he couldn't get a rescue team together until later this evening. And that would be too late.

Ella lowered herself to the ground next to Garrett. At least they were together. The wet ground seeped through her skirt. Ella bit her lip to keep from crying. Hopelessness gripped her soul.

"*Nichts ist jemals so hoffnungslos, wie es scheint.*" *Nothing is ever as hopeless as it seems.* Oma's words whispered in her heart.

Then why do I feel so hopeless?

She caressed the bandage on top of Garrett's head, then leaned down to kiss the narrow area of skin on his forehead.

So von Kirchbach wouldn't help her – even though he wouldn't be alive now without her assistance. Ella cringed at the irony of it all.

If he wasn't going to help, then she would have to help herself and Garrett, but how? She needed a plan.

St. Gertrude, pray for us. Holy Souls in Purgatory, pray for us. Pray for Garrett. Pray that I will not lose hope in this situation. Pray for a miracle. Please, God, help us.

Her mind searching for a plan, Ella climbed to her feet and wiped her muddy hands on her skirt. The chain of her shackle bumped her apron and made a little clunk sound. As if she had something in her pocket. Certain that she'd put nothing in it, Ella reached into her pocket and her fingers brushed two items. She yanked them out, and her heart began to beat with hope as she stared at the key and little slip of paper in her hand with the words:

Dieser Schlüssel dies befreit Sie und Ihren Verlobten. Pferde in der Scheune. Gehen Sie um 11:30 Uhr. Nur eine Wache im Dienst. Zerstöre nach dem Lesen. Geben Sie den Schlüssel in den Wassereimer in der Nähe der Scheune zurück WvK

(This key will release you and your fiancé. Horses in barn. Go at 11:30. Only one guard on duty. Destroy after reading. Return key to water bucket near barn. WvK)

Her hand flew to her chest and she gasped. Could it be? After all that fuss, von Kirchbach *was* allowing her and Garrett to escape, and for that she would be forever grateful.

Wanting to share the good news, she looked down at Garrett. His broken body immediately reminded her of the other POW officers she'd seen. What about them?

Her hands still shaking, she inserted the key into the shackle and, after a few attempts, released both her and Garrett. Ripping up the note into as many pieces as she could, she dug a hole in the ground and buried the papers deeply.

It was 1120 hours, so she worked quickly.

Now, she would need help. After unshackling them, she would ask for Dolan's and the Southerner's assistance. They could help her bring Garrett to the barn and lift him onto a horse, and she could ride the mile or so to the field hospital in Roubaix. The two conscious men could escape into the forest.

Next, she would make sure the unconscious men were unshackled.

Ella needed to give him hope. "I'll be right back, Garrett. We're going to escape." He stirred in response to her words.

She opened the flap of the tent and peeked out. The shadow of a guard was only a stone's throw away, so she ducked her head back inside.

Ella waited a few moments and opened the flap again. The guard was nowhere to be seen. She snuck out of their tent and into the tent with the two conscious men. They glanced up at her with open mouths.

"I have a key," she whispered and held up the key. "I'll need one of you to help me with Corporal Brown."

"Where did you get a key?" Corporal Dolan asked.

"It doesn't matter. Please, I need your help." She crouched and unlocked both shackles, then gave the key to the man with the Southern accent. "Sir, could you please sneak into the tent beside this one and unlock the chains of the other prisoners, then bring the key back to me?"

"Sure thing, ma'am." He took the key and limped his way outside.

She helped Corporal Dolan stand up. It was the first time she saw a clotted gash at the side of his head.

"You're hurt."

"It can wait. Please, let's help Corporal Brown."

Ella peeked outside the tent ensuring no guard was near, then she and Dolan stepped outside and quickly into Garrett's tent. With Dolan's help, Ella pulled Garrett to his feet. He moaned, then his body flopped to one side and Dolan caught him before he fell. Wrapping their arms around him, they dragged him out of the tent.

Chapter Twenty-Seven
Escape

Did he hear her correctly? *Did Ella just say "escape?"* Either that, or he was dreaming. How in the world –

Garrett's world shifted. Hands latched onto his arms, his shoulders—the pain!—and lifted him to his feet. Unable to stand on his own, he slumped to one side, but someone caught him. In the next instant, his arms were draped over two figures, one shorter than the other. Lilac perfume. Ella? How? What was happening?

Outside now. They dragged him under the open sky, his feet scraping the cold ground, renewing the pain.

Outside? No, he wasn't ready to go. He needed something...important...mission. "My...cap, where's...my cap? Must have...my—"

"I'll get it," Ella said.

Within a moment, they were pulling him again. His feet felt like lead weights and his head pounded, but Ella's perfume and calming words soothed him.

The stench of horse manure wafted by his nostrils. He cracked open his eyelids to find himself leaning against a horse and Ella fiddling with the reins. "Corporal Dolan is going to help you onto the horse, Garrett. He and another soldier were with you in the *camion* after you were captured."

Ella and the man named Dolan whispered. Garrett felt

himself being lifted onto the horse. "My...cap..."

"Yes, I have that, Garrett."

Ella pressed her hands to his bottom, then Dolan grabbed his underarms, and they hefted him onto the horse's bare back. Ella mounted in front of him, and he flopped his arms around her waist. Still unable to hold himself up, he leaned his head on her shoulder. If he didn't make it, it was worth being this close to her.

***

She sat there, holding onto the reins and contemplating. Checking her timepiece, she was surprised. 1158 already? They'd run out of time, but with Garrett semi-conscious, Ella needed to find a way to attach him to her. She twisted and saw that Garrett wore a muddy belt. Could that work? No, she needed something longer and sturdier. She scanned the barn and spied a rope hanging from one of the hooks.

"Corporal? Could you grab that rope for me and tie it around both of us?"

"Yes, Miss."

Dolan tied the rope around the two of them in a crisscross shape over both her and Garrett's chests and pulled it uncomfortably tight. He seemed to be making some sort of a knot that hopefully wouldn't come undone.

Before she could thank the corporal, sounds of a door slamming and rustling behind them made her straighten.

"Looks like one of the guards and a woman," Dolan whispered. He pulled the horse and himself back into the shadows and the two of them waited. Ella's heart was beating so hard, she thought it might explode right out of her chest.

A woman's giggling and a man's lowered voice became distant.

The corporal patted the horse and whispered, "Looks like *Frau* Hoffmann and the guard are taking a stroll. They didn't appear to see us."

Ella allowed herself to breathe, and willed her heart to stop thundering in her chest. She finally managed to whisper to Dolan. "Thank you, Corporal."

Before she took another breath, a branch cracked just outside the barn. Ella froze. *Please, not another guard.*

A figure came into view. It was the Southerner. "All 'em shackles are undone, ma'am."

"Good," she said, blowing out a sigh of relief.

"Yes'm," the Southerner replied. "I had to wait to come because a man and a lady were strolling by."

"Yes." Ella paused. "Do you have the key?"

"Yes'm." He held it out.

"Please put it in the water bucket just outside the barn."

The man disappeared for a second then returned.

"Now," she said to the two young men, "get going. Avoid the area near the farmhouse. There's only one guard at this time, and he's there." She pointed. "A forest edges this area for miles." She pointed out the doors of the barn. "That should keep you safe for a while. The town of Roubaix is right over the border that way. "

"Yes'm," the Southerner said.

"Thank *you*, sirs."

"No, thank *you*, Miss," Dolan's voice came from somewhere behind her, but she didn't dare twist around to make eye contact. The footfalls of both men faded as they ran out of the barn and, she hoped, towards the forest.

All right, God. I know You're there. Please help me get Garrett to the field hospital. St. Jude, St. Gertrude and Our Blessed Lady, please pray for our safety.

If this was going to work, she had to make the quickest getaway she could with this horse. "Hold on tight, Garrett." Ella clicked her tongue until the horse began to move, and she was out of the barn.

She yell-whispered, "Yah, yah," kicked the horse's sides hard and went into a gallop. For a moment, she could only hear the wind and galloping of the horse.

But less than a minute later, distant noises came from behind her. She couldn't think about that. Shots rang out, and she prayed that Garrett wouldn't get hit by a bullet. They wouldn't chase after her for one man, would they?

Distant sounds of motors revving and the realization that vehicles or *camions* were likely following made her kick the horse harder. She thought of nothing else, only riding that horse until they reached the hospital in Roubaix. Clutching the reins, she focused on the galloping rather than the motorcars. All those afternoons of racing her horse against the ranch-owner's daughter were paying off.

The rope securing Garrett in place dug into her chest and started to cut off her breathing, but she couldn't stop, especially since the lights of Roubaix were ahead of her. She had only three-quarters, maybe one mile, before she reached the field hospital there.

The field hospital was within sight when a *camion* ahead swerved across the road and blocked her way.

Ella hadn't come this far to get captured. She tried to maneuver around the truck, then saw a very tall man – *Collins!* – waving at her. She pulled the horse to a stop. "Whoa," and the two of them, still connected by the tight rope, nearly fell off and onto the ground. She held firmly to the reins and straightened just in time.

Collins rushed to her side. "Miss Neumann, this wasn't within your purview to –"

"I had to, sir. Garrett and two others were scheduled to be executed at noon. We need to get Garrett to the field hospital up ahead." She paused. "There are five more men who need rescuing, Lieutenant, and two Allied men in the forest as well. If you want to take Garrett, I shall go back and –"

"No, you take him to the field hospital. When you didn't return, I went immediately to Roubaix and got six volunteers from the field hospital. They're in the back of this *camion*. We were on our way to rescue you and Garrett when we saw you coming. Besides, our intel told us where we'd find you."

"Your what?"

"Look, time is of the essence. How many enemy soldiers are at the camp?"

"My last count, I believe it was around five, including Major von Kirchbach, the commandant, and not including Frau Hoffmann."

"Very well, thank you. Then they're outnumbered." He paused. "Do you have Garrett's cap?"

"Yes, yes, I do."

"Please give it to me."

She took the cap out of her apron pocket and handed it to him.

Collins then took what appeared to be a photograph from the top of the cap. "Thank you. Now take the major to the field hospital."

"Yes, sir."

Chapter Twenty-Eight
British Red Cross Hospital

When Ella rode up to the British field hospital in Roubaix, three soldiers pointed guns at them and ordered them to halt.

She raised her hands. "We're Allies. Please let us through. This man is an Allied officer in urgent need of medical attention."

The soldiers shook their heads. One said, "Why in blooming 'ell 'air you dressed as a German nurse?"

"Lieutenant Collins from Le Tréport sent me to the POW camp on the other side of the Belgian border. Please, I am an American nurse. I am from Philadelphia, and I've been working at the stationary hospital in Le Tréport. Please!"

One man tilted his head; another narrowed his eyebrows in suspicion.

"Can ye prove it, Miss?" one of the men asked.

She dropped her hands, exasperated. "How?"

"Name the capital of the largest state in the United States?"

Ella sighed. At least they didn't ask a difficult question. "That would be Austin, Texas."

The one man glanced at the other, who nodded.

"Very well, come on in." Their weapons dropped to their sides, and they waved her in.

They had some difficulty untying the knot that connected Ella and Garrett – obviously Dolan had done an excellent job. Even with the rope loosened, she could barely breathe, and the rope had caused a sizeable brush burn on her skin. But it was well worth it to bring Garrett back safely.

When they finally untied and untangled the two of them, stretcher-bearers took Garrett away, and Ella took the deepest breath of relief she could muster.

***

Garrett's eyelids felt like dark, heavy curtains. Was someone clamping them shut? But he no longer rode on a horse; he was on a cot. He felt a kiss to his forehead. *Ella.*

"You're at a British field hospital in Roubaix. You're... going to be fine." Her voice, soft and consoling, was on the verge of breaking. She gently held his left hand, bandaged and sore from the wounds. If only he could open his eyes. Instead, he tried to squeeze her hand to let her know he heard her.

He drifted in and out of consciousness. The pain in his head lessened and his stomach, though still sore, didn't ache as much, and even his hands felt better. However, his jaw felt like it had been cracked open and put together again.

Someone coughed, and Garrett finally managed to open his eyes. There, at his bedside – or more appropriately, partly on his cot – sat Ella. Her eyes were closed, and her head rested beside his wrapped hand. She had already washed and changed into her usual nursing uniform. He tried to take a deep breath, but it felt like someone was stabbing him. *Broken ribs.*

He took his left hand and placed it on top of her head.

She bolted upright and squealed. "Garrett! You're awake!"

He nodded. The pain in his jaw kept him silent. He was sure he'd sound like a simpleton if he tried to speak.

And yet the expression in her eyes when she realized he was conscious was worth any broken bones, ribs or head injuries he had suffered.

"I was so worried about you."

He tried to smile, but the pain in his jaw – and a bandage around the lower part of his face – prevented him, so he squeezed her hand.

***

Ella's heart swelled with joy. Since she and Garrett had arrived at the small field hospital, he had been operated on for his wounds, and then he hovered on the edge of unconsciousness for nearly twenty-four hours. She shifted in her seat. Her chest, legs, and behind were bruised and sore after horseback riding and being tied to Garrett. But any pain she endured was worth the joy she felt.

Before Garrett woke up, the doctors informed her that he had suffered a concussion, and there were five deep lacerations to his head that needed suturing. His skull had been fractured. Four ribs were cracked, and his jaw was broken, but they had set it in the OR. They also told her that recuperation after head wounds was impossible to predict, but they had every reason to believe he would be fine.

"I'm so sorry, Garrett."

He nodded.

"I know that you couldn't have told me everything." She hesitated. "The doctors said you should be well enough to be transferred to Le Tréport in a week or so."

Garrett opened his mouth to speak and grunted. "C...ca..." He closed his mouth, frustration coloring his expression.

"Ca? Oh, your cap? Yes, Collins asked for it. I gave it to him. I hope that's all right. He took a photograph from the top of it."

He nodded, then his eyes began to close.

"Wait, before you go back to sleep."

He opened his eyes wide.

"The answer is yes."

His eyebrows lifted, in a look of confusion in his eyes.

"You said you wanted to marry me, remember? The answer is yes."

He tried to smile again. His eyes brightened with joy.

"I love you, Garrett."

He squeezed her hand.

"I'm going to let you sleep now. I shall be back shortly."

She waited until he closed his eyes, then she made her way to the other side of the barrack to check on the rescued and wounded Allied officers. Two teetered on the edge of death, but so far, none of them had succumbed.

Lieutenant Collins and his men were able to capture the POW camp and rescue the Allied officers. She wanted to ask him where the German POWs had been taken, but she didn't have an opportunity to ask him. She hoped von Kirchbach was being treated humanely. After all, he'd helped them escape.

Finding it stuffy in the hospital barrack, Ella opened the door. A breath of fresh air and perhaps a cup of coffee or tea would refresh her. As she stepped outside, she nearly ran into a young man.

"Excuse me," he said.

Then she glanced up into the face of Corporal Dolan.

"Miss Ella!"

"Corporal! You made it!"

"Yes, we did. You made it easy actually. Since the enemy was trying to catch you, they didn't even come looking for us. We made it here a few hours after you did."

"Where's the Southerner?"

"Oh, he's just enjoying the company of the British medical volunteers. They claim his accent is 'adorable.'"

Ella laughed.

"What's his name, Corporal? I shouldn't be calling him the Southerner."

"His name is Private First Class Junior Jones, from Mississippi."

"Well, I'm so glad Private Jones is enjoying his stay here at the field hospital."

"And by the way, my first name is Patrick."

"And you may call me Ella. Thank you, Patrick, for your help. I couldn't have done it without you."

He lowered his head. "It's I who should be thanking you, Ella. We'd be executed by now if you hadn't intervened."

Ella leaned in to hug him and kiss him on the cheek.

Dolan's pale face flushed a bright red. He cleared his throat. "You... saved my life... and probably the lives of the other men. If there's ever... anything I can ever do for you, please let me know. I promise to do it if it's within my ability to do so."

"No need, Patrick. Besides, a promise is kind of what got me into the situation."

"How so?"

"I'm afraid the information is classified. But someday, I'll share the story with you."

"I look forward to that day." Patrick Dolan winked at her.

Chapter Twenty-Nine
Unexpected Delivery

While Ella waited for Garrett to recuperate, she offered her services to the field hospital. Besides, now that the doctor was confident that Garrett's head injury would heal, Ella felt enough at peace about his injuries that she could spend her energy helping others. For the first day, she worked where Garrett was, in the barrack for newly wounded, but then she was asked to clean and do laundry and other duties. It wasn't surgery, but she was nonetheless happy to be contributing.

On her way to dump a basin of dirty water, a female cried out from the other side of the surgical tent Ella passed. Ella put down the basin of water and met a girl as she was rounding the corner of the tent. She had seen the girl before, a young, big-boned girl, who wore a blue uniform with white apron but no red cross. Ella assumed she was a French volunteer.

"What's wrong?" Ella reached a hand out to offer assistance.

The girl tilted her head and squinted. Ella tried to remember the French words. "*Qu'est-ce qui ne va pas?*"

The girl then spoke so quickly that Ella couldn't understand her. Finally, she said, "Hurt," then, "*Je souffre.*" The girl grabbed her middle and moaned.

Behind her, the doctor stuck his head out of the surgical tent. "What's wrong out here?"

"The girl needs help, doctor, but I can't understand what she's saying because she's speaking so quickly. She's in pain."

He asked her in French what was wrong. She replied in rapid-fire sentences, and the doctor said, "The girl must have the flu or something. Take her to one of the barracks to see if you can figure out what's wrong until I'm finished here in the OR."

"Yes, sir."

Ella wrapped an arm around the girl's shoulder to calm her. "It's all right. *C'est bien.*" As they walked, Ella asked the girl, "Name? *Nom?*"

The girl replied, "Renée."

"*C'est bien, Renée. Je... vais vous aider.*" Right about now, Ella wished she was more fluent in French.

Ella escorted Renée to a smaller barrack.

Several tidy cots lined one wall, all but one empty. The lone recuperating soldier glanced up from the book on his lap.

Ella guided the girl to the nearest cot, glancing around for a nurse but not seeing one.

Grabbing her belly, the girl winced and moaned. Ella scanned the barrack for a dressing screen to give the girl privacy. She spied one near the exit on the other side of the barrack, picked it up and brought it closer to the girl. The soldier in the cot had put down his book and was watching Ella.

When Ella set up the screen, she helped the girl remove her apron and skirt. When Renée was down to her shift, Ella said, "I'll need this off too so I can examine you." She helped the girl slip out of her shift and gasped. The girl's stomach was...so large. *Oh, Lord, she's pregnant! Could she be in labor?*

Ella had never delivered a baby before, and she was guessing perhaps the girl didn't realize she was pregnant. "Renee, um...*bebe?*"

"*Quoi?*" Renee asked.

"*Bebe.*" Ella pointed to the girl's stomach and repeated, "*Bebe.*"

The girl's face blanched, and she spoke too quickly for Ella to understand.

Ella needed to get someone in here who could speak French and translate for her.

She peeked around the dressing screen. "Sir, do you speak English?"

"Yes, ma'am, I do," he answered in an Australian accent.

"Are you ambulatory?"

"Am I what?"

"Can you walk?"

"Yes, ma'am."

"Would you mind searching for a nurse who speaks French? I need someone to assist me! Please hurry!"

The man got up and although he had a limp, he was able to move quickly as he exited the barrack.

Ella lowered Renée down to the cot and tried to determine how far along she was. Obstetrics wasn't Ella's specialty, but she vaguely remembered her youngest sister's birth, and if there were no difficulties, delivery could be pretty straightforward.

Renée reclined against the pillows. Ella went to the wash basin and scrubbed her hands and elbows as well as she could. She would need something sharp to cut the umbilical cord. Above the wash basin she found a metal kit, and inside, a pair of scissors. From behind her, Renée grunted.

Ella covered her with a blanket and positioned herself at the foot of the bed. Her mouth fell open.

Renée looked ready to push. She cried out, "*Qu'est qui ce passe?*"

"*C'est un bebe, Renée.*"

"*Quand?*"

"*Maintenant,*" Ella shouted. Her hands trembled. Glancing over her shoulder, she prayed that someone else might come. Pushing past the nervousness, Ella rubbed the girl's leg.

A woman came into the barracks saying—in French, thank God—in a loud voice, "It will be okay, my dear, just relax." She pulled up a chair next to Renee's head and grabbed her hand. "You'll do fine, my dear. Take a deep breath." The poor girl probably hadn't had time to process what was going on.

"*Merci,*" Ella said to the nurse.

"No worries," the nurse responded in English with a British accent. "My name is Sr. Martha. I'll stay with you."

"Thank you."

Since Ella was already sitting at the foot of the cot, she remained there. Sr. Martha said something in French to Renée, probably directing her to give one more push. Within minutes, the baby's head, covered with black hair, was crowning.

"Stop pushing," Sr. Martha told Renée in French.

The baby soon slid out onto the cot, a baby with dark black hair, tiny – perhaps five and a half pounds – but crying and breathing. It was a girl!

Sr. Martha waited a few moments before she cut the umbilical cord. Then she gathered the baby in a blanket, and turned her attention to Renée. In French, Ella assumed that she told Renée to give one more push to deliver the placenta. Sr. Martha took the crying baby to the sink.

Sr. Martha called over her shoulder. "Once the placenta is delivered, lay it out flat to make sure it's intact to confirm it came out in its entirety."

"Yes, Sister," Ella responded. The placenta slipped out, and Ella carefully laid it out flat on newspaper on the floor to make sure nothing was missing from it.

Sr. Martha, holding the swaddled baby girl, glanced downward at the placenta. "Looks like it's all there."

The now-quiet baby was placed in her mother's arms. Ella couldn't imagine what it would be like for a new mother to give birth with no preparation or warning. Warning or not, this baby was a beautiful gift.

Sr. Martha helped Renée to breastfeed her daughter. Ella couldn't stop staring in awe at the wonder of this brand-new life.

Amid this wretched, horrible war that had already killed and maimed millions, this tiny life filled Ella with overwhelming hope and joy.

When Ella sutured wounds and repaired injuries, she often worked in a race with death. But this – *this* was the miracle of new life, welcoming into the world a new human person made in the image and likeness of God.

Ella had never felt so alive as when she helped bring this new life into the world.

Did she still *want* to be a surgeon? Could she be both? Weren't obstetricians also surgeons?

"*Merci, mademoiselles*," said Renée, gazing at Sr. Martha and Ella.

"*Non, merci, Renée,*" Ella said, grateful that she was able to help accompany this new life into the world, and it had given her a perspective she may never have had otherwise.

Perhaps she was meant to change her medical specialty.

Chapter Thirty
Return to Le Tréport

Garrett, after a few days of rest, was grateful that he was well enough to be transported to the stationary hospital at Le Tréport.

While at the POW camp and even during his torture, he had resigned himself to the fact that he would be executed. Whenever he regained consciousness, he prayed that God would spare him.

Thankfully, Ella hadn't given up on him. Although she was on duty, Ella did manage to find an hour each day to spend time with him. He hadn't yet been able to speak, but he could nod yes or shake his head no. And he could also write questions on a pad of paper. From the way Ella described it, the entire escape seemed somewhat miraculous. She had said, "Well, I had a little help from someone whose life I saved, as well as the assistance of the good corporal and private here. And we must not forget the agreeable, speedy horse and the many saints I was petitioning."

He also listened in amusement as she shared with him the story of delivering Renee's baby. The way she spoke, her entire face shone. Even before she had told him, Garrett knew Ella well enough to know that she was likely going to change her specialty to obstetrics.

On the ambulance ride on the way to Le Tréport, Ella

accompanied Garrett and six other soldiers. Garrett sat upright beside Ella and two other ambulatory patients, one of whom was a Corporal Dolan. Although Ella had introduced them earlier, he had forgotten the other man's name. Guessing from his accent, he was a Southerner, and they all acted like old friends. Garrett liked them well enough, but the look in Dolan's eyes said he was smitten with Ella and would probably like to be Ella's beau. *Get in line, Dolan.* Besides, Ella was *his* girl so Dolan would have to look elsewhere.

As he watched Ella talking with the other soldiers, he was more certain now that he was meant to spend the rest of his life with her. She was not only lovely and kind, she was smart, brave, and capable of espionage-level operations.

***

When she returned to work, Ella was pleased to discover that Sr. Nora was gone, and Sr. Gladdie had taken over her duties. At least working conditions were more tolerable.

On the 11th day of the 11th month at the 11th hour, the war officially came to an end. However, news of the armistice didn't reach Le Tréport until later that day.

Garrett was now ambulatory and when the bells rang at Le Tréport, Ella found him in the dining hut. They embraced. "It's over! The war is finally over, Garrett!"

"Thank God," he said.

Now that the war was over, Garrett's transformation from Corporal Brown back to his true identity as Major Smith would mean that his hair didn't have to be dyed and he no longer had to wear glasses. He was now missing two bottom teeth, but Ella assured him it wasn't very noticeable.

Ella had already shared with Garrett the story of the baby's birth and that she'd like to study surgical obstetrics instead of general surgery.

It had been a chilly, wet day, but as the afternoon progressed, the sun came out, and the remaining orange, red, and yellow leaves on the trees swayed in appreciation. Wounded soldiers and medical personnel alike emerged from their barracks and clapped and celebrated the end of the war.

Horns honked, music played outside and in the tents. Medical volunteers and recuperating soldiers shouted, sung, laughed.

Everyone smiled and walked with a bounce in their step. Ann and Clara joined Ella and Garrett. They were planning on attending the cinema that night since a Charlie Chaplin film would be showing.

At dinner, they filed into the dining hut nearest the main building. The din of the crowd made it difficult to think. But then again, they *were* celebrating. They had just sat down when Ella noticed Sr. Nora walking towards her with a determined step. Ella hadn't seen the elderly woman in nearly three weeks.

The elderly woman stopped beside Ella. Garrett stood. Ella avoided eye contact and stared at the woman's feet shifting from one to the other.

"Nurse Neumann?" her raised voice carried over the noise of the many people in the dining hut.

She finally glanced up. What she saw surprised her. Sr. Nora wasn't frowning. Nor were her eyes glaring at her. Sr. Nora placed a hand on Ella's shoulder. "May I speak with you for a moment" – she glanced at the others – "privately?"

"Of course, Sister." Ella walked with Sr. Nora to the area near the doorway.

Ella remained quiet, her back to the door, waiting for Sr. Nora to speak.

"Nurse Neumann?"

"Yes, Sister?" She tried to make eye contact with the elderly woman, but Sr. Nora's gaze was on Ella's apron.

"I... owe you an apology."

Ella's mouth fell open, and she straightened but said nothing.

Sr. Nora finally made eye contact. "I...well...I allowed my prejudice... to get in the way of doing my job." She paused. "You've demonstrated your surgical skills. You've also shown great courage. I hope you can find it in your heart to forgive me for the way I've treated you."

Her tone and voice were kind and her eyes were glassy with tears.

Ella paused before speaking. This woman had been the bane of her existence over here, but now she was asking for forgiveness. She took hold of the elderly sister's hands. "Of course, Sister. I do forgive you."

"You're very kind, Nurse Neumann. Thank you for unburdening my conscience."

Not only was today a day to celebrate the end of the war, but Sr. Nora's apology filled her heart with compassion and mercy. Ella embraced the woman.

After a moment, Sr. Nora stepped away. "Two of my dearest nephews were killed in this blasted war. I hadn't realized how much hatred I've been harboring for the enemy. It took a long conversation with a priest to realize I have much to atone for."

"Thank you so much for coming to see me. I really do appreciate it."

As Ella turned to leave, Sr. Nora gently tapped her on the shoulder. "Lieutenant Collins asked to see you when you've finished your lunch."

"Of course."

Back at the table, Ella shared Sr. Nora's unexpected but heartfelt apology with Garrett, Clara, and Ann. She ate her soup and bread quickly, then excused herself to meet with Collins.

She nodded to his secretary, then knocked on Collins' door.

"Please come in."

Ella swung open the door. A tall, thin woman sat straight in one of the two chairs across from the desk. Collins stood up as Ella entered and motioned her to sit in the other chair.

"I'd introduce the two of you, but you've already met."

Ella turned in her seat to face the woman, who said, "*Guten tag, Fraulein Müller.*"

"Frau Hoffmann?" Ella's mouth fell open.

The woman laughed. "Actually, it's Mrs. Mary O'Brien. I'm from Dublin, but my parents were German. Like you, I grew up in a bilingual house and can speak the language fluently."

"So *you* were the person on the inside of the POW camp."

"Yes."

"I can't believe it." Ella playfully nudged her. "You were very convincing."

"As were you, Nurse Neumann."

Collins cleared his throat. "Well, ladies, I just wanted to make sure the two of you met, now that the war is over. Nurse, please don't share this information with anyone else. Even though the war is over, the enemy doesn't know Frau Hoffmann's true identity."

"Of course. Thank you, sir," Ella stood up.

***

Back at the dining hut, Ella could hardly sit still with all the excitement. The war was over. Sr. Nora had apologized. Frau Hoffmann was an Irish woman working for the Allies. And she and Garrett would spend the next few months here in Le Tréport together before going home.

She took hold of Garrett's hand and bid goodbye to Clara and Ann.

Outside, as they strolled along the walkway, a large, shimmery, blue butterfly flew in front of them. Ella's eyes widened as the stunning butterfly swooped down on them once again. Butterflies in November? The intense, shining bright blue color of the insect seemed supernatural. Butterflies meant new life and now that the war was over, new lives would begin.

Chapter Thirty-One
Christmas in France

Ella took the temperature and pulse rate of a young, unconscious soldier, then wrote down the notations on his chart. Two weeks ago, this poor fellow had been injured when he stepped on a live land mine which had exploded. Although he was alive, he had no legs, and had remained unconscious for the past two weeks.

There were six other men in the ward, mostly critical and all unconscious.

When the war ended six weeks ago, Ella had assumed that her duties would be less clinical. But since she was one of the small number of medical personnel who had remained, she was busier than ever. And of those who had stayed – like Clara and Lieutenant Collins – she would likely never see them again, but they would all share the bond of this sacrifice in common.

She glanced up at the evergreen wreaths with green and red glass ornaments that adorned the barrack. Ella's heart tightened. They were all expected to go to work tomorrow, Christmas Eve. This was the first time she felt so far away from home. In Philadelphia, her mother would be making cookies and cakes and other treats for the season. Her family would be attending Midnight Mass tomorrow evening at St. Peter and Paul's Cathedral in Philadelphia.

Garrett's smiling face came to mind, and her heart leapt with joy. He had promised her that he would take her to Paris by train for Midnight Mass.

The door opened, and she turned. It was Garrett, and he smiled from ear to ear. "Ella, it's snowing!"

"That's wonderful."

"Come, see." He took her by the arm.

"Wait, my coat!" She lifted her coat off the hook, put it over her shoulders, and followed him outside.

When she stepped outside, Ella was surprised by how much snow had already fallen. There was at least two inches – maybe more – on the ground. That was one of the drawbacks of the tent barracks: no windows.

Just as she was putting on her gloves, a snowball careened into the side of Garrett's face.

Ella giggled. Lieutenant Collins laughed as he was the one who had thrown the snowball. She was so pleased to see the tall man laughing, as she'd never even seen him smile.

Garrett gathered snow into a very large snowball and when Collins wasn't looking, he tossed it at the big man, and it hit him on the back of the head. He turned and gave a mock frown, then smiled.

A flash of snow hit her arm. Ella looked up to see Clara laughing. The girl stood beside Collins, and her small stature truly made him look like a giant.

Ella made her own snowball and tossed it at Clara, but Clara ducked, and it missed her.

Despite her homesickness, Ella's heart was filled with joy. These people had become her family. They had shared more in nine months than most families shared in a lifetime.

When they stopped tossing snowballs, Collins clapped his hands and gathered everyone around. Although they were scheduled to work the following day (Christmas Eve), Collins told them they could all begin their holidays a day early.

Collins then specifically approached Ella and Garrett. "Just a minute, Major, Miss Neumann. I've got some news for both of you."

"Oh?" Garrett asked, taking Ella's hand and moving closer to Collins.

"News...for both of us?"

"Miss Neumann, I have arranged for you to be readmitted to Woman's Medical College of Pennsylvania in Philadelphia. I believe you attended one semester before you left?"

Ella straightened. Had she heard him correctly? "Yes, I did, sir. But I'll be here until February."

"You and Major Smith are to be discharged after the new year. The second term for first-year medical students begins on January 15."

Her mind reeled, and her heart raced. She was going back to medical school! She turned toward Garrett.

Grinning from ear to ear, he pulled her into an embrace and kissed her forehead. "This is such great news, Ella."

So happy she could burst, Ella leaned back to look him in the eyes. "It is! I'd been wanting to finish medical school."

He stroked her hair, joy radiating from his eyes. "This is really happening. It's your gift, your calling."

A happy little laugh escaped her. She loved this man. He was being discharged with her! She couldn't wait to start life with him. "I had planned on working a few years first. It's so expensive, I didn't think..." As the cost of such an education dawned on her, her joy fizzled. She faced Collins again. Another little sacrifice had presented itself. "Sir, I cannot even begin to thank you for your assistance in getting me back into medical school, but I wouldn't be able to... well...pay for the tuition."

"My dear, it's my pleasure. You're a talented young nurse, and you shall be a talented physician." He reached out and shook her hand.

Did he not hear her? She wouldn't be able to pay for the tuition. "Thank you, sir, but—"

"No buts. You don't have to worry about the tuition. A private donor will be paying for your medical education."

Ella's eyes widened. "What? Is that true?"

"Yes, it's true."

"Who?" she and Garrett asked.

"I'm not at liberty to say."

"Well, how am I to thank them?"

"I'm sure he – or she – knows you're grateful."

Grateful? She placed her hand on her chest. This morning, she had no idea how she would finish medical school without money. Garrett had told her that God would provide. Well, God had provided and had inspired someone to generously provide for her education. She felt beyond blessed.

Could it be one of the men whose life she saved? There were a few who came to mind: von Kirchbach, the soldier in the operating theater, the men in the POW camps. But who could possibly have enough money to fund an entire medical education?

Garrett saluted Collins, then the two men shook hands. Collins walked off.

Ella pulled her coat closer around her. Under her wet gloves, her hands trembled. She peeled the gloves off and shook them to get rid of the snow and dampness. She put them back on.

Garrett put his arm around her shoulder and kissed the top of her head. "Well, that's excellent news, Ella. I'm so proud of you."

"I still can't believe it. I wonder what my parents will say when they find out I'll be returning to college."

"They'll be happy. But they might be even happier when they discover you have a betrothed."

"We'll see about that, Major Smith."

***

In the dining hut, Ella and Garrett sat drinking hot cocoa. Just about everyone from the camp was there. Someone had chopped down a small pine and had decorated it with glass balls and stringed popcorn. Boughs of evergreens hung on the door and walls. People were laughing, the mood festive. As happy as she was, Ella wondered how they would get married while she was in medical school.

Garrett reached across the small table and squeezed her hand. "Penny for your thoughts? You're quiet."

"How can we get married *and* how I can manage medical school?"

"That's easy. We wait to get married until *after* you've completed medical school."

"That's three years away. I don't want to wait."

"I don't really *want* to wait that long either, but becoming a doctor is important to you. And because of that, I'm willing to wait." He leaned forward and whispered, "Love is patient, love is kind." He kissed her cheek, released her hand, and sat back in his chair. He winked.

Ella released a deep, gratifying sigh. This man was certainly not like the average man, who might've insisted she *not* complete medical college.

"Besides," he said, "waiting will help me to be more patient. We can still see each other and get to know each other. I'll look for employment in Philadelphia. I can teach history at one of the high schools."

"Yes." She took a sip of cocoa. "I'll be 25 years old then. You won't mind marrying a spinster?"

"Well, we'll be formally engaged during that time."

"Of course."

He leaned in and kissed her cheek.

The next evening, they attended Midnight Mass in Paris. Ella's heart rejoiced as the choir sang. She had already been given many gifts. The war was over. She now had a plan for her life. She would be attending medical school, then marrying Garrett after a three-year courtship.

***

When they emerged from Midnight Mass in Paris, a soft misty snow had begun to fall. She buttoned the top of her coat. Garrett held his arm out, and Ella took hold of it as they strolled to the hostel.

Behind them, the bells of Notre Dame rang out with two bongs.

Garrett stopped walking. "Merry Christmas, Ella." His breath made a puff in the air.

"Merry Christmas, Garrett."

When they reached the Paris hostel where they were staying, they went inside and took off their coats and hats. When Ella turned toward the staircase, Garrett took her hand and pulled her to him. "I haven't yet given you your Christmas gift."

"Then you must allow me to go upstairs to my cot and get your Christmas gift."

"Of course."

Ella raced up the stairs, trying to be as quiet as she could under the circumstances. On the second-floor women's section, she raced to her cot, reached into her bag, and took out the two small gifts for him.

She returned to find him standing in the parlor in front of the fireplace. He placed a log on the hot coals and adjusted it with a metal poker. A moment later, he stood and faced her. "That was fast."

The fire raged in the fireplace bathing the parlor in a warm, orange glow. A little Christmas tree stood in the corner, glass balls and bits of silver tinsel decorating its branches, but no lights.

"Come." He took her by the hand and guided her to the sofa by the fire.

He knelt before her, and pulled out a small brown package from his pocket. "Merry Christmas, Ella."

She unwrapped it to find a small velvet box. She lifted the lid. On a black velvety cushion sat a modest diamond ring in a gold setting. The diamond caught the firelight and flashed as she gazed at it. Her heart melted and glowed, knowing the love this ring represented. It was simply beautiful.

"I've already asked you to be my wife, and you've said yes. With this ring, I want to make it official."

"Garrett, this is so lovely."

"I wish it could've been a bigger diamond."

"It's just right." She slipped it over the ring finger on her left hand. It fit perfectly. "How did you know what size ring I wore?"

"A little espionage work. You know, I have extensive experience in that."

"Well, I'm surprised." She leaned close to him and kissed him on the lips. "Now, it's my turn." She reached into her skirt pocket to produce the two small boxes. She held out the larger of the two gifts. He unwrapped it. He read the cover of the book out loud. *A Pocket Book of Military Poems.* He smiled widely.

"Read the inscription."

He opened the first page and read aloud. "To Garrett, Merry First Christmas, 1918, Love Always, Ella." He blinked. Were his eyes watery?

"This is beautiful, and I will treasure it, Ella. Thank you so much."

"Do you really like it?"

"Yes, I do. It's perfect, and the inscription means everything to me."

"This is our first of many Christmases together."

"The first of many, indeed."

"One more." She handed him the second box which was small, but not as small as the ring box.

"I have no idea what this could be."

"You don't? That's good."

Garrett held the box in his hand. He shook it, and the contents of the box clunked against the side of the box.

"What could be moving around in there?"

"Open it!" She bit down on her lip and clasped her hands together.

He lifted the top off the box and laughed out loud. "This is perfect!" Inside the box were four stones of differing colors and a note indicating where each stone was retrieved and what date.

Merry Christmas, Garrett! These are pebbles I picked up while we were together.

You already have a shiny light blue-green stone that I picked up near Lille, August, 1918.

Black-speckled gray pebble, September 30, near cinema, Le Tréport hospital grounds.

Red stone with hole, October 15, near POW barrack.

Blue-green stone: November 25, Mers-les-Bains, day-trip to Mers-les-Bains

Pink stone: December 2, Le Tréport, near Terrace of Funiculaire

They sat on the sofa for several minutes, the crackling of the fire, Garrett's breathing and the beating of her heart the only sounds.

He hummed "Silent Night." She wished she could stay like this all night, but it would be frowned upon for an unmarried couple to do so.

Ella was grateful for this beautiful Christmas and such a hopeful end to a year that had begun with her enlisting to be a medical nurse. Images of the most horrible wounds she had ever witnessed came to her mind: gaping chest wounds, faces blown off, limbs torn off, gas burns, not to mention the way she found Garrett and the others in the German camp.

And yet after suffering comes joy and hope for the future. She recalled Renee giving birth to her little baby girl. In only three years, Ella would be a trained obstetrician. And...she would also have opportunities to use her surgical skills.

She gazed at the crucifix on the wall above the fireplace. Without the crucifixion, there would be no resurrection. Without the suffering, there would be no joy and hope.

"I love you," Garrett whispered and kissed her cheek.

"I love you," she responded, wishing that this moment could last forever.

Epilogue
Three Years Later
June 17, 1922

It had been a long – and sometimes tiresome – three years of studying obstetrical surgery and practical medicine. Ella and Garrett had spent every Sunday together, beginning with Mass at Saints Peter and Paul Cathedral in downtown Philadelphia, then lunch at her parents' house. Thankfully, Garrett had obtained employment at Roman Catholic High School for Boys, teaching History and German.

Ella was scheduled to begin her first year of internship in August at the Cortland County Hospital in upstate New York. This hospital had sought her out and offered her an internship and residency because they had just opened a new maternity ward. The offer included maternity leaves (or ones that she hoped to have in the future) and a generous salary as well as a house. She would no longer live near her family, but the rural area of Cortland appealed to her.

But now, as she stood at the back of Saints Peter and Paul Cathedral, she could not believe she and Garrett were finally getting married.

Ella adjusted her lacey veil as she and her father stood at the back of the cathedral. After her teen sisters, Frida and Maria, processed down the aisle, her four-year-old nephew Rudolph, as the ring bearer, followed them. The organist played the wedding march, and the people in the church stood. At first, she moved at a reasonably slow pace, but then she started walking more briskly. Her father pulled on her arm to slow her down.

The aisle seemed longer than she remembered. Of course, she had never walked down this aisle before as a bride.

Faces in the crowd smiled back at her: Ann, her co-worker and friend from France, and her husband, Theo. High above the crowd, she saw Lieutenant Collins' beaming face. But she wasn't prepared for the rush of emotions when she saw Garrett standing straight, his mouth wide in a smile from ear to ear, dressed handsomely in a formal morning suit. Beside him stood his brother, Hank, and beside his brother was her brother, Frank, who winked, which finally made her chuckle.

She and her father made it to the front of the church, where her father gave her arm to Garrett's outstretched hand.

The priest began, "*In nomine Patri, et Filii et Spiritus Sancti. Amen.*"

***

The luncheon reception was held at the Roman Catholic High School Hall, and a local restaurant provided the meal for the hundred guests. After the reception, she and Garrett would stay one night at a small hotel here in Philadelphia, then they would take the train to Cortland, then to Niagara Falls for a two-day honeymoon.

At the reception, Ella tried to speak to each person who came to the wedding from afar, so she barely had time to eat. Some traveled as far as Kingston, Ontario and upstate New York. Great-Aunt Eva came from Germany. Ella felt it only right to spend as much time with each guest as she could.

She and Garrett first sat and spoke with his parents, Mr. and Mrs. Schmidt, along with Hank, his brother. Garrett's parents had changed their surname back to Schmidt in the aftermath of the war. Garrett and his brother decided to keep their surname as Smith. Garrett's parents, both with quiet personalities, seemed to enjoy speaking with Ella in their native language. His mother, a big woman, seemed to adore Ella. The affection was mutual.

Ella had encouraged Garrett to visit his parents as frequently as possible. She had only been able to accompany him once in the summer of 1919, and his mother had made Ella feel like part of the family immediately.

After kissing Garrett's parents, they moved on to a table with some of their co-workers from the war, including the former Surgeon-Lieutenant Collins, Ann (Fremont) and her husband, Theo. She chatted with Ann and Theo for a few moments, then turned to Collins, who stood as she approached. The man completely filled the area when he stood, and she was reminded how handsome he was. He took her hand and kissed it. "Congratulations, Mrs. Smith." His low voice was warm and friendly.

"Thank you, sir."

"I understand," he said, "that you've completed medical school, and you'll be moving to Cortland, New York."

"That's correct. It's quite exciting."

"I'm very pleased it all worked out so well."

"Yes, although I wish I knew who so generously financed my education so that I may thank him...or her."

He leaned over and whispered in her ear, "You just did, Mrs. Smith." He straightened, and she lifted her chin to see a wide smile across his face.

She stepped back and tilted her head. "It was *you*?"

He nodded.

Ella leaned toward Garrett. "Did you hear that? Lieutenant Collins was my donor."

Garrett's eyes widened, then he laughed. "That's almost like hiding in plain sight, sir."

"First, it's now Dr. Collins. And, second, I did have help from my friend, Sr. Nora."

Ella's mouth opened, but she couldn't speak. Then she tentatively smiled as the news of the identity of her donors sunk in. "What? You...uh...you and Sr. Nora – but why? How?"

"I was born into wealth, and it was only when I joined the Army that I realized that not everyone has it so easy. I decided to give away some of my wealth to help others. Before she left Le Tréport, Sr. Nora found out what I was planning to do and asked if she could contribute."

"Well, I'll never be able to thank you enough, sir. Do you happen to have Sr. Nora's address in England?"

"I thought you might want that." He handed her two cards. "One of these cards is from Sr. Nora. Her address is on the card. This one is from my wife and me."

She took both cards from him and handed them to Garrett, who put them in his pocket.

Collins shook Garrett's hand, then faced Ella. "And the way you can thank me is to be an excellent physician."

"I will certainly do that, sir."

He smiled widely. "And someday, perhaps you can contribute educational funds for someone else."

"Most definitely, sir."

A waiter approached Garrett and Ella. He held a tray of filled wine glasses. "Sir? Madam?"

Garrett took a glass from the tray and handed it to Ella, then he took a glass for himself. He sipped, then asked Collins, "Where do you live now?"

"It's interesting that you ask."

"It is?" Garrett tilted his head in an expression of confusion.

"Yes, I live and work in a small town in Upstate New York called Cortland."

Ella gasped. Garrett sprayed a bit of wine from his mouth.

"Cortland?" Ella asked.

"Yes. I will be your new employer."

"I can't believe it!" Ella would not be working for a stranger.

"I need you in the new maternity ward. I knew you would take the job offer if I added time off for any maternity leaves you might take and other benefits."

"Why didn't you just tell me?"

"I wanted to surprise you."

"Well, you've done that."

"I look forward to working with you, Mrs. Smith."

"Likewise, sir."

Collins lifted a glass to them, winked and returned to his table.

On their way to the next table to speak to guests, she whispered to Garrett, "Can you believe that?"

He shook his head.

As they passed her parents' table, Ella pulled on Garrett's arm. Her feet ached from standing for the past hour or so. "I'm going to sit for a bit with my mother."

He let go of her hand, and she took a seat beside her mother and her great-aunt, Oma's only surviving sister, Eva Rabold. Ella's family had only just met her the previous night.

At age 75, Eva was a spinster, but even at her age, she was beautiful, her face, smooth and pale, and devoid of any deep wrinkles. She wore her white hair pulled up in a chignon. Ella had learned that Eva had come to the USA for the wedding and an extended visit.

"How do you like Philadelphia, Aunt Eva?" she asked in German. A waiter came around with wine, and Ella held up her glass while the man poured. "Thank you."

The woman lifted her shoulders and replied in German, "It's fine. I didn't want to come here but my niece's husband, Johann, convinced me, told me I needed to see more of the world."

"Johann?" Ella knew little about that side of her family, only that Rabold was Oma's maiden name and that she had four brothers and two sisters.

"Yes. Johann told me that I could represent the Rabold clan at the wedding."

"Wonderful. Well, I'm so happy that he convinced you to come and to have finally met you." Ella took a sip of wine.

"The feeling is mutual, dear," the older woman said. "By the way, his son, Wilhelm, served as an officer in the Great War and was even captured and told me about a pretty American nurse who saved his life."

Ella's eyes narrowed, and she almost brushed off her curiosity. "Wait. What's Wilhelm's last name?" she asked in English, then remembered that Aunt Eva only spoke German, so she asked the question again in German.

"Von Kirchbach."

Ella gasped, choking on her wine. For a moment, she couldn't speak, her mouth gaping. Her mother and Aunt Eva both asked her what was wrong.

"Well, nothing...is...wrong. It's just...."

The two women leaned closer to Ella.

"I'm...well, *I'm* the nurse who saved his life."

Aunt Eva clapped her hands together. Mama laughed out loud and in German, she said, "You saved your cousin's life?"

"Yes, I did!" She paused. "And he saved Garrett's and my life. Remember I told you about that, Mama."

Mama nodded.

Ella's heart still thumping, she asked Aunt Eva if she had Wilhelm's address, to which she answered yes.

"May I have it? I would enjoy writing to him and letting him know we are related."

"I'm sure he would also enjoy it, dear," said Aunt Eva.

Her hands still shaking, Ella returned to Garrett to share the news that von Kirchbach, whose life she saved, was actually a blood relative.

Like Ella, Garrett's mouth fell open, but he said nothing. Finally, he shook his head. "You were obviously in the right place at the right time."

"Indeed I was."

***

Garrett squeezed his wife's hand as they sat on the

moving train. He enjoyed travelling by train because of the mountain scenery. They had just stopped in Scranton to pick up passengers, then it would be on to Binghamton, New York, and then on to Cortland. He found this particular trip more enjoyable because his wife was with him. After three and a half years of courtship, sometimes it seemed like 1922 would never come. It finally did, and now they would be together for the rest of their lives.

Ella's voice was high-pitched. "I'm so grateful to be married to you and to be here on this train and to not be studying!"

"I am too, love."

"I still can't believe von Kirchbach and I are cousins."

"Yes, that was quite a surprise."

"And that Lieutenant Collins – I mean, Dr. Collins – will be my employer."

"That too." *And those won't be the last surprises you'll receive, my dear,* he thought.

After a short trip to Cortland, and a two-day honeymoon in Niagara Falls, Garrett arranged for a surprise visit to Kingston, only a three-hour train ride from Niagara Falls. Of course, Ella assumed that they would be visiting his parents and brother, because they had just returned home from the wedding. But that wasn't the main purpose for this trip.

It was a beautiful, warm and sunny day when they arrived in Kingston. Garrett hailed a cab. Birds sang sweetly in the trees. A group of children squealed as they played tag. A few men mowed their lush green lawns. The idyllic scene bore no trace of the war. Garrett thanked God that the Great War had been over for more than three years.

The taxi pulled up to a majestic brick home by the water. Figures stood on the lawn: two men, three women and a few toddlers. Garrett got out and assisted Ella from the vehicle. She squinted as she stared at the couples. "Oh, my, Garrett, I can't believe it! This is a wonderful surprise!"

***

"Julia, Ann, Charlotte!" Ella raced across the lawn and embraced the three women. *Is there no end to the surprises this week?* As she embraced her friends, Ella felt the presence of little children nearby.

"It's so wonderful to see you again, Ella," said Ann, as her toddler son, George, clutched her dress. "You are still glowing."

"Thank you. I'm so glad you were able to attend the wedding, Ann."

"It was a beautiful wedding, Ella." Ann leaned over and picked up her son.

"Where is Theo?"

"He couldn't get away. But I just couldn't miss this wonderful reunion! And it's so easy to travel by train these days. We're fortunate to be living in such modern times."

"You're right about that, Ann."

Ella turned towards Julia, whose eyes glistened. Julia held her hands to her face in wonderment, her stomach large with child. "Ella, you haven't changed a bit. You look absolutely lovely. Congratulations on your graduation and your wedding! I'm so sorry we couldn't attend. But, as you can see, I'm quite far along with our second child, and Peter didn't want to risk traveling."

"I understand completely. When is your baby due?"

"Yesterday." Julia patted her belly.

"Oh, dear." Ella laughed.

Ann stepped forward and pointed. "Well, if anything happens, you're in good hands with Dr. Kilgallen present."

"What about Ella, Ann?" Julia asked.

"Of course, Julia. You'd also be in good hands with Ella."

"Right! We were all surprised to hear that you're now an obstetrician." Julia smiled widely.

Ella waved her hands as if to dismiss the idea. "I'm surprised I didn't have to search for a job."

"Yes, and Cortland is closer to here than Philadelphia."

"It is. And we'll be near Garrett's family here in Kingston."

A dark-haired boy screeched as he played with a man Ella assumed was Peter Winslow, Julia's husband, dark-haired and handsome. "That's our first child, Pete Jr. He's very loud."

"I can tell," Ella laughed.

Charlotte waved her hands. "I'm not so sure that Pete is louder than my daughter, Colette, Julia. That's Colette over there with my husband, Paul. We'll do proper introductions later, Ella." A brown-haired toddler girl squealed as her father tickled her and lifted her in his arms. He approached Garrett. Julia's husband, Peter, picked up his son and followed as the men shook hands and warmly greeted one another.

It occurred to Ella that many gentlemen these days acted so formal and proper that they didn't interact much with their children. It was a refreshing sight to see these men enjoying fatherhood.

The women left the children with their fathers and ambled to the circle of lawn chairs in front of a beautiful brick home and sat down.

Once they were all seated, Charlotte spoke. "It's such an honor to have you all with us today. To be relaxing here on this beautiful day, to be surrounded by new life..."

Julia cleared her throat, then said, "It's hard to believe it's three and a half years since the war ended. But I have to say... the war – and God – taught me to trust in God more than myself. Life truly is a 'gift'."

Ann chuckled. "Like all those gifts you had saved for your beloved?"

"Yes, indeed."

"Beloved?" Ella asked.

The girls recounted how Julia had bought or made Christmas gifts for her future husband many years before she had met him. Then, when she *did* meet him, she didn't think Peter *was* her beloved.

"Well, obviously, I changed my mind and our son over there and this little one here" – she patted her stomach – "are proof of that love."

The young women nodded in unison.

"And the war taught me" – Charlotte straightened in her chair – "that life is a gift up to and including the moment of death," she paused and lowered her head, "And even then, we can be present with each dying person and make sure they know how much they are loved."

For Ella's sake, Charlotte then recounted how she discovered her true calling by spending time in the terminal ward at the field hospital in Vauxbuin and holding dying soldiers' hands and singing them into eternity.

"That's beautiful, Charlotte," Ella said.

"What did the war teach *you*, Ella?" Charlotte asked.

Ella paused before responding. She hadn't reflected much on the war since it ended. But thinking about it now, there were too many things to share. "Well, the most important one is that joy isn't possible without sacrifice and suffering. We wouldn't be able to celebrate the Resurrection without the Passion of Christ."

"Well said, Ella." Charlotte gently squeezed Ella's hand. Of all the women there, Ella had only spent a brief time with Charlotte on the ship over to France, but now she felt a deeper bond with her.

"And," Ella continued, "after racing against time to save men from death, I realized that I wanted to be part of welcoming new life." Of course, Ella understood that in obstetrics, maybe she would still at times face death too. She thought of her two brothers who died as toddlers – but certainly that wouldn't be a daily occurrence.

Just then, the little dark-haired girl – Colette? – ran to her mother. Charlotte lifted her onto her lap. "You mean welcoming this little dolly here?" Charlotte asked and kissed Colette's cheek.

***

Garrett shook both Peter Winslow's and Dr. Paul Kilgallen's hands. He had met both these men at the field hospital in Vauxbuin near Soissons when he had been injured while undercover as a German officer. Of course, Peter had been his Allied liaison in that area, but it had been a long time since he had seen him.

Garrett followed Peter and Paul as they walked to the side of the house and gazed out at the beautiful lake.

"Sorry that we had to miss the wedding, old boy," said

Peter. He patted Garrett on the back. "But Julia is quite far along."

"I'm kind of happy you didn't come," Garrett offered.

"What?" Peter asked.

"It's not like that. Because you didn't come, I decided to arrange this surprise trip so we could all spend time together. I'm quite thankful to you, Dr. Kilgallen, for your hospitality and for allowing us to have our little reunion here."

"It's Paul, please. Happy to help. Besides, Charlotte was very excited about planning the entire affair."

"Good." Garrett paused. "How are the two of you enjoying married life?"

Peter spoke first. "Immensely, especially if you compare it to war life. I often wonder why I survived when so many perished."

"I agree," said Paul. "However, those who died would want us to live our lives."

"Yes, they would," Garrett said. "Yes, they would."

***

On this beautiful day, Ella was thankful for her husband, for her family, and for her wartime friends. As they chatted and laughed, children's squeals sometimes interrupted their conversation, but the sounds were so sweet that Ella wished she could make a vinyl record to keep them forever. She hoped and wished that someday, she and Garrett would have giggling children of their own.

Ella relished the sounds, their friendships, and her overflowing joy, but she would never forget the men and women who gave their lives during the Great War. She prayed that there would never again be such a horrific war.

"The year's at the spring
And day's at the morn.
God's in His Heaven –
All's right with the world."
(Stella Maris, 1918)

Poems and Prayers

"Prayer of a Soldier in France" *(1917)*

First appeared in *A Treasury of War Poetry (1917)*

Sergeant Joyce Kilmer (1886-1918)

My shoulders ache beneath my pack
(Lie easier, Cross, upon His back).
I march with feet that burn and smart
(Tread, Holy Feet, upon my heart).
Men shout at me who may not speak
(They scourged Thy back and smote Thy cheek).
I may not lift a hand to clear
My eyes of salty drops that sear.
(Then shall my fickle soul forget
Thy Agony of Bloody Sweat?)
My rifle hand is stiff and numb
(From Thy pierced palm red rivers come).
Lord, Thou didst suffer more for me
Than all the hosts of land and sea.
So let me render back again
This millionth of Thy gift. Amen.

"I Have a Rendezvous With Death" by Alan Seeger

I have a rendezvous with Death
At some disputed barricade,
When Spring comes back with rustling shade
And apple-blossoms fill the air—
I have a rendezvous with Death
When Spring brings back blue days and fair.

It may be he shall take my hand
And lead me into his dark land
And close my eyes and quench my breath—
It may be I shall pass him still.
I have a rendezvous with Death
On some scarred slope of battered hill,
When Spring comes round again this year
And the first meadow-flowers appear.
God knows 'twere better to be deep
Pillowed in silk and scented down,
Where love throbs out in blissful sleep,
Pulse nigh to pulse, and breath to breath,
Where hushed awakenings are dear...
But I've a rendezvous with Death
At midnight in some flaming town,
When Spring trips north again this year,
And I to my pledged word am true,
I shall not fail that rendezvous.

St. Gertrude's Prayer for the Holy Souls

Eternal Father, I offer Thee the Most Precious Blood of
Thy Divine Son, Jesus, in union with the masses said
throughout the world today, for all the holy souls in
purgatory, for sinners everywhere, for sinners in the
universal church, those in my own home and within my
family. Amen.

Acknowledgments

Special thanks to the Arnprior and District Museum (Cathy Rodger) for lending us the vintage clothes to photograph the cover. Thank you also to Jamie Bentz for being such a patient cover model.

Thank you to Theresa Linden for the excellent job of copyediting. This book would not be nearly as polished without your keen eye. Special thanks to Dr. Jean Egolf, Dr. Michael Wahl, and Dr. Barbara Golder, for helping me with medical terms and procedures. To Ann Frailey, Nick Lauer, Sarah Loten, and Carolyn Astfalk for proofreading and helpful editing advice.

Thank you to my good friend, Ingrid Waclawik, for making sure the German in this novel was correct.

Again, my gratitude to Ian Frailey for coming up with the series title: Great War Great Love.

I'm incredibly grateful to my husband, James, for listening patiently as I shared plot lines and character studies and for helping me to develop the story and characters. Also thank you for your cover designs for all three books of the series. I literally could not have done this series without you!

Last, but certainly not least, my gratitude to God and to my deceased parents, for giving me life and for inspiring me to write religious fiction.

About the Author

Ellen Gable (Hrkach) is an award-winning author (2010 IPPY Gold medal, 2015 IAN finalist), publisher (2016 CALA), editor, self-publishing book coach, speaker, NFP teacher, Marriage Preparation Instructor, Theology of the Body teacher, and past president of the Catholic Writers Guild. She is an author of ten books and a contributor to numerous others. Her novels have been collectively downloaded over 700,000 times on Kindle and her books have nearly three-quarters of a million pages read on KDP. She and her husband, James, are the parents of five adult sons, seven precious souls in heaven and grandparents to one adorable grandson. In her spare time, Ellen enjoys reading on her Kindle, researching her family tree, and watching live-stream classic movies and TV shows. Her website is located at www.ellengable.com.

Ellen enjoys hearing feedback from her readers: please email her at fullquiverpublishing@gmail.com

Published by
Full Quiver Publishing
PO Box 244
Pakenham ON K0A2X0
Canada
http://www.fullquiverpublishing.com/